Arthur
The Legend Unveiled

By
Christopher Johnson
&
Eve Lung

Illustrations by Karen Saul

Arthur
The Legend Unveiled

©1995 Christopher Johnson & Eve Lung

ISBN 1 898307 61 X

Cover design and illustration by Daryth Bastin

Published by:

Capall Bann Publishing
Freshfields
Chieveley
Berks
RG20 8TF

This book is dedicated to

MINERVA

who made herself known one summer
in Tintagel

About the Authors

Eve Lung is a seer and teacher of Celtic and Native American shamanic traditions.

Christopher Johnson is a post graduate student of social and political thoughts and a fan of Carlos Castineda.

Acknowledgements

Many thanks to Pam Ellis for typing the Introduction and to Karen Saul for typing the remaining draft manuscript and for her beautiful illustrations.

Also our thanks to Calvin Powell for his connections and to Pauline Powell for retyping the manuscript for publication.

Contents

ii

INTRODUCTION

Arthur's World

King Arthur was born at Tintagel in Cornwall in about 450 AD. The date is, unfortunately, an approximation for there is actually little reliable historical evidence to confirm either his birth or the events of his life. Many of the earliest sources, such as the 'Saxon Chronicles', do not mention him at all and other sources only mention him in passing.

The stories about Arthur that we are most familiar with today were not written until at least five or six hundred years after his birth and in any case they were not really designed to be taken as literal historic fact.

The closest we can come to the actual historical figure of Arthur is that he was most likely the Celtic Chief or King who succeeded in turning back the onslaughts of invading Saxon hordes in about 490 AD. A warrior named Arthur led a series of battles against the invaders and, after a final encounter at a place called 'Mons Badonicus', the

Saxons were defeated. They withdrew to the coastal areas of the South and remained subdued for some 60 years, giving Britain some much needed rest.

Although we may not know very much about the historical Arthur we do know a great deal about the world into which he was born and his world in the middle of the 5th Century was a very troubled time indeed.

Britain was in a state of political, social and religious turmoil. For three and a half centuries the land had been ruled by the Roman Empire. The Romans, bringing with them their own version of civilisation, managed to change a social structure that had been developing slowly but surely for thousands of years.

Before the Romans had arrived, the land belonged to the Celts, as indeed did most of mainland Europe at one time. The Celts seemed to have originated in the mountainous areas of Europe which are now known as Austria and Switzerland. Gradually as their numbers increased they expanded into France, Germany, Britain and Ireland where they eventually developed a more settled way of life.

They organised themselves into different tribes, each having its own distinct territory with chieftains, an aristocracy, farmers and craftsmen. Although the tribes frequently fought amongst themselves they had much in common with each other including a common language and a religious tradition that stretched right back to the dawn of humanity.

The Celtic craftsmen were skilled ironworkers famous for manufacturing weapons such as the double edged sword and beautiful highly prized pots or vessels known as cauldrons. The Celts also produced good quality wool, pottery and exquisite jewellery and ornaments made from precious metals especially gold.

The British Celts were fortunate for gold was to be found in Ireland, copper in Wales and tin in Cornwall. Over a period of time trading links developed between the tribes of Britain and those of mainland Europe and the British Celts began to prosper.

They prospered to such an extent that by about 55 BC the Roman Empire became very interested in the British Isles and Julius Caesar mounted an armed expedition to survey the land as a prelude to invasion. The Roman Empire was always in need of good arable land in order to feed its towns and its enormous standing army. It was also always ready to relieve other people of their wealth because running a vast empire was an expensive business.

Caesar had plenty of first hand experience of the Celtic nations because he was at that time in the process of conquering Gaul (Celtic France). He knew for instance that they found it difficult to act as a cohesive fighting unit because they were too fond of quarrelling amongst themselves - "too much given to faction" as he put it. However, there was one thing about the Celts that Caesar paid particular attention too and that was a class of people within Celtic society that he called "Druids".

Very little is known today about the Druids, but they seem to have been a kind of religious order, made up of women as well as men, who officiated at religious rituals and other ceremonies. It has been suggested that they may have played an important organisational role within the gold trade since most of the gold produced was destined for decorating religious offerings.

Apart from religious duties the Druids were also royal advisers, custodians of the laws and traditions of the land, judges and last but not least, magicians of the highest order. Unfortunately none of their knowledge or tradition was written down because the Druids relied solely upon oral learning for the transmission of their culture. It must have been an arduous apprenticeship for it sometimes took as long as twenty years for a prospective Druid to acquire the necessary skills and knowledge. They were a powerful class of people who seemed to have operated beyond or above the confines of individual tribes and territories. This is clearly demonstrated by the fact that they used the Isle of Anglesey in Wales as a base and here they organised druidic conventions and colleges of learning which attracted Druids from all over the Celtic world.

Since none of their knowledge was in written form most of what we know about them comes from what others, notably the Greeks and the Romans, have written about them. The word 'Druid' itself comes from the Greek and seems to be derived from something meaning "knowledge of the oak" or "great or deep knowledge". Caesar disliked the Druids intensely and depicted them as people who conducted barbaric sacrifices to their gods. This is the image that survives today in the minds of many people - grisly rites at dawn amongst the oak groves or defenceless scapegoats burnt alive in enormous wicker baskets. It is hard to counter this image because there is such a lack of information especially from the Druids themselves.

Two things stand in their favour, however. Firstly, the Romans could hardly consider themselves above barbarism when they were in the habit of throwing live people to lions in order to provide popular entertainment, when they executed thousands upon thousands of people by grotesque methods such as crucifixion or when the foundation of their very civilisation itself was based upon the degrading practice of slavery.

Secondly, Caesar's comments about the practices of the Druids are hardly likely to have been unbiased observations. He knew that the Druids, educated, intelligent, well esteemed by the people and largely above tribal rivalries, were the one class of people who were capable of co-ordinating serious mass resistance to an invasion. The man was halfway through conquering Gaul and was obviously planning to do the same to the British Isles. He therefore needed some kind of justification to obliterate the Druids because of their political potential.

Julius Caesar was denied his dream of conquering Britain, however, because fortunately or unfortunately, he was murdered not long after his return to Rome and the Empire had to wait until 43 AD before it could fulfill its mission. When the Romans returned they managed to subdue the South of Britain and began establishing towns like London and Colchester. They met with serious resistance from some of the Celtic tribes, the leader of one of them, Caractacus, managed to withdraw towards the Druid stronghold of Anglesey and waged guerrilla warfare before being betrayed by a Celtic Queen from a rival territory.

Following Caesar's recommendations, the Roman commander Suetonious, was determined to crush the

Druids and their influence. He marched his forces towards Anglesey and in AD 60 he crushed it, destroying the sacred groves and most of the Druidic organisation.

While this was happening, however, (and this clearly illustrates why the Romans were so interested in Britain), the Roman Procurator, Catus, moved against the Iceni tribe led by Queen Boudica. Boudica's husband had recently died and had left half of a vast fortune to the Empire in the hope that his family and tribe would be left in peace. Catus, however, wanted the other half. When Boudica resisted she was flogged and her daughters raped. Determined to seek vengeance, Boudica raised an army and marched south. She sacked London, St Albans and Colchester and destroyed the 9th Legion before being finally defeated by Suetonious and the remaining legions.

The rebellion crushed, the Romans began the process of colonisation. Prosperous trading centres developed with houses, schools, baths and temples while in the countryside life revolved around large luxurious, self-sufficient villas which were usually isolated from the ordinary villages. Latin became the official language. A network of military roads soon criss-crossed the land linking together garrison forts built on the edges of the Empire to stop the unconquered tribes of the north and those from Ireland from wreaking havoc. Some of the tribes within the Roman boundaries managed to keep a kind of independent identity and some measure of local government, but as time wore on more and more people began to value the status of Roman citizenship and the old political structure and values were abandoned.

Other Celtic traditions suffered less. Having crushed the Druid order the Romans were quite happy to leave the actual religion of the Celts more or less alone. As was their custom in other occupied countries they began to identify the Celtic Goddesses and Gods with their own Roman versions. For instance, the Celtic Goddess Bridgit became equated with Minerva the Roman Goddess as did Sulis the Celtic Goddess of the healing waters, and a brand new temple was built at Bath to accommodate Her worship. Celtic religion then was not suppressed merely Romanised and as the iron grip of the Empire began to firstly relax and then crumble, the old Celtic ways began to reassert themselves. By the mid 4th Century new temples were being built where the Goddesses and Gods were known by their old names once more.

By this time, however, another new element was being introduced into British society. The Emperor Constantine had been converted to Christianity in 312 AD and he was determined to make it the official religion of the Empire. It is not known exactly when Christianity made its first appearance in Britain but by 314 AD there were enough Christians about to send a small delegation of bishops to a council at Arles. It seems likely that the wealthier members of society converted to Christianity when it became the official religion in order to make sure of their own personal status as Roman citizens.

Archaeological evidence demonstrates how the new cult began to develop. For example, at Lullingstone in Kent followers of the Old Religion and a new Christian group seem to have shared the same premises. Silchester in Hampshire has an early Christian church built in the 4th Century as well as four temples to the Old Religion (which is quite impressive for a community of just over 2,000 people!). In 1963 a mosaic pavement (now in the British Museum) was discovered in a field by Hinton St

Mary in Dorset. The mosaic shows a combination of Old Religious and Christian themes and according to John McNeill, an author who has written extensively about early Celtic churches, there are many other instances where rudimentary artwork has been used to portray the old pagan mythological figures in an obvious Christian context. So even at this early stage Christianity was making a concerted effort to draw people away from the Old Religion into the new one!

The coming of the Roman Empire then brought a new social and political order to a land which had been politically and socially stable for well over a thousand years. It brought a new language and eventually a new religion. When the Empire finally collapsed and the last of the legions withdrew in 410 AD they left behind them a social and political vacuum which had to be filled as quickly as possible.

Some would-be leaders attempted to continue a Roman-style government but without the backing of an actual Empire this proved impossible. One man, Constantine, declared himself Emperor and taking with him all the available fighting men he could, marched towards Rome never to be seen again leaving Britain almost undefended.

All through the occupation the unconquered northern tribes had been constantly harassing the Romans - which is why Hadrians' Wall was built. With the garrison forts now unmanned these Scots and Picts streamed across the border at will taking crops and driving off cattle. The Irish began raiding in earnest from the west and, as if this was not enough, from the south came an even greater threat. Saxon invaders started to drive out the Celts. To begin with these Saxons had been welcomed and hired as mercenaries to fight the Picts and the Scots. After a while, though, it became clear that they were looking for new territories in which to settle. Wave upon wave of invaders came across with their families from the region of Europe now known as Germany. These Saxons and Angles were savage barbarians compared to the now Romanized, civilised Britons. They were brutal and much feared.

The Britons had no option but to fall back upon their old pre-occupation styles of government in order to prevent chaos. The Celtic system of kings or chieftains with independent territories was quickly restored. The Latin language, which had never been used much by the majority of the population anyway, was dropped in favour of the old British tongue (except by the Christian Church of course!) and a fight for survival began. Thousands of native Celts were themselves forced to emigrate to Armorica (Brittany) as the Saxons pushed westwards.

This then was the world of turmoil into which the young Arthur was born. The stability of the old way of life had been broken by the Romans, a new vigorous religious cult was threatening the Old Religion and weak fledgling systems of government were trying to cope as best they could with invasions from all sides. By the time Arthur was a young man the Saxons had captured a large part of the south-east of the country and were threatening Cornwall. Indeed they may have already arrived for according to the Welsh 'Chronicle of Tysilio' Arthur's' father, Uther Pendragon, was poisoned by them.

Chapter One

According to legend King Arthur was born at Tintagel in Cornwall. His father, Uther Pendragon, was King of all Britain and his mother, Igraine, was the former wife of Gorlois, Duke of Tintagel. Uther fell in love with Igraine the first time he saw her and was determined to make her his wife. He managed to kill Gorlois in battle and that night before Igraine learnt of her husband's death, Uther enlisted the aid of Merlin the magician and assumed Gorlois's likeness in order to sleep with her. This is how Arthur was conceived. Shortly afterwards Uther and Igraine were married.

Now in order to gain Merlin's assistance in the first place Uther had agreed to hand the child over to him as soon as he was born and so Merlin took Arthur away. He left him with a Knight called Ector, and Arthur grew up in his household believing himself to be Ector's youngest son.

When Arthur came of age, Merlin arranged a contest between the nobles of the land to discover who should be the rightful King. Using his magic he set a sword in a large stone and upon the stone was an inscription which said that whoever drew the sword from the stone was the rightful King of England.

Arthur was the only one who ever drew the sword from the stone and so Merlin proclaimed him the rightful King.

The other nobles were not satisfied by this test, however, and they rebelled against Arthur's rule; it took several years of hard fighting and much help from Merlin before Arthur was recognised as King throughout the land.

This is how the legend of Arthur began. It is the version that most people are familiar with and is taken from the works of one Thomas Malory, a Knight who lived in the 15th Century. He produced a collection of stories about Arthur and had the honour of having his work printed by Caxton's press in 1469 under the title *Le Morte d'Arthur*.

Most of what we take for granted now about Arthur, his Knights and their adventures, the round table, the search for the Holy Grail and so on, is based upon this one, rather large collection of stories. Malory's version of the legend may well be the best known version but it is by no means the original, indeed even Caxton's preface to the 'Morte - d'Arthur' acknowledges that Malory borrowed his material "from certain books of the French".

What Malory actually did was to bring together for the first time in one work the enormous amount of material that had been written about Arthur during the previous four centuries.

Malory, if you like, produced the definitive version and because it was all contained in one collection and also had the benefit of being actually printed, it was immediately much more accessible to the public than the manuscripts of the previous centuries and people became much more familiar with his version than with the other stories.

To continue, briefly, the story along Malory's lines, Arthur, with Merlin's aid, was soon able to establish himself and began a golden reign. He gathered around himself a body of loyal knights and Merlin made a round table for them to signify equality amongst them - no one could sit at the head of the table and claim to be more important than the others.

After a while Arthur decided to take a wife and chose Gwenivere, against the better judgement of Merlin, who advised against the match.

Arthur broke the sword that he took from the stone in a duel with the Knight Pellinore and Merlin took him to a lake where a mysterious fairy lady dwelt. From her hand Arthur received Excalibur, the best sword in the land - a magical sword which could never be broken. Its scabbard too had magical properties, its wearer would never bleed to death.

Soon after Arthur and Gwenivere were married, this same fairy, known as the Lady of the Lake, lured Merlin away from Arthur's court and imprisoned him in an ice cavern where he remained. A new Knight appeared at the court, Sir Lancelot; he was an excellent fighter and quickly became King's champion. When Gwenivere was kidnapped it was Lancelot who set out to rescue her and the two fell in love.

In the meantime, Arthur's half-sister, Morganuse, seduced him without Arthur's knowledge of who she was. She bore a son called Mordred. His other half-sister, Morgan Le Fay, was an enchantress. She stole Excalibur and its scabbard, leaving a fake copy in its place and tried to get her lover to kill Arthur with his own sword. When this treachery was discovered she persuaded and helped Camille, another enchantress, to assume the likeness of Gwenivere and sleep with Arthur.

Meanwhile, the real Gwenivere was with Lancelot. Morgan Le Fay, who was in love with Lancelot herself, captured him and kept him prisoner in her castle but he managed to escape. She took out her revenge on Gwenivere and made it known at the court that Gwenivere had been unfaithful to her husband Arthur.

Thus over time these and other instances led Arthur and his Knights away from the high moral standards that they had once achieved. A kind of corruptness set in and desolation fell upon the land. In order to restore the Kingdom to its former glory the Knights set out to search for the Holy Grail. The Holy Grail was the cup that caught the blood of Jesus as he was dying on the cross. It was also the cup that was used by Jesus in the last supper. Joseph of Arimathea, the man who buried Jesus, brought the cup to England and took it to Avalon. This was the only thing that could save the Kingdom but its whereabouts were unknown. One by one the Knights searching for the Grail failed and died. Only Sir Galahad, (Lancelot's son by Elaine) was 'pure' enough to be granted a vision of the Grail and ask the question "Whom does it serve?".

Galahad, because of his purity, was able to fulfil his Grail Quest and the land was restored. Gwenivere and Lancelot went to France to escape but Arthur followed to bring

Gwenivere back, leaving Mordred in charge of the Kingdom. While Arthur was away, however, Mordred raised an army and proclaimed himself King. Arthur returned home and faced Mordred at the battle of Camlan. Mordred died and Arthur was himself mortally wounded. He was taken away by boat to Avalon and Excalibur was returned to the lake once more.

This then is the story of Arthur that most people know and accept. In it he is the rightful King of England, and brings peace and plenty to the land until corruption sets in. The idyll was ruined by the ungodly behaviour of the Knights and the court and Arthur's own inability to stand against them. There was too much frivolity, jealousy and squabbling; too many extra-marital liaisons (especially where Lancelot and Gwenivere were concerned) and general un-Christian behaviour.

The land suffered as a result and could only be restored by a 'pure' Knight seeking and being granted a vision of the 'Holy Grail'. Even when the land was restored Arthur could not escape the consequences of his own 'sins' and was in the end defeated and killed by his own illegitimate son, Mordred.

This then is a very brief account of the legend of Arthur according to Thomas Malory, as mentioned before, however his account is not the original version but a compilation of the works of others.

In producing his own version, Malory necessarily made changes. He edited the stories, he left out long sections here and there, he altered names to make the stories fit together better and often emphasised different points in order to suit his own purposes. The original stories were often very different, and in particular they did not have the distinctly Christian overtones that characterised Malory's version.

Stories about King Arthur were first brought to public attention in 1135 when Geoffrey of Monmouth produced a book called 'A History of the Kings of Britain'. It could well have been called 'A History of King Arthur', since almost a third of the work is devoted to him. Some years later, Geoffrey also wrote a poem entitled 'Vita Merlin' which told of the life of Merlin the magician.

It is taken for granted nowadays that Geoffrey's books were more romantic than factual (he has Arthur conquering almost the whole of Europe), but Geoffrey claimed to have based them on a much older source, which unfortunately has proved untraceable. It seems very probably, however, that a body of oral tradition existed long before Geoffrey's account and it is highly likely that he was well acquainted with this source. In addition a number of very early Welsh poems mention Arthur a great deal, poems such as 'The spoils of Annwyn', written well before 1066, and 'Culhwch and Olwen' (taken from a collection known as the 'Mabinogion') which goes back to at least 800 AD. It seems reasonable to suppose then that Geoffrey based his account upon knowledge or tradition already in existence long before he started writing.

Once Geoffrey had produced his 'history' an avalanche of works about Arthur and his court began to appear. Writers and poets reworked the basic story and added their own elements and interpretations. Wace, in 1155, shows Arthur as an heroic figure and introduced the idea of the round table (in his 'Roman de Brut').

The French loved Arthur and added the more romantic courtly elements to the legend. Chrètien de Trôyes wrote *'Lancelot'*, *'Percèval'*, *'Yvain and Cliges'* between 1170 - 1190. Chrètien was responsible for introducing the Grail theme for the first time, thus opening up a more spiritual dimension which was quickly followed and added to by Robert de Boron in 1190. De Boron retold the Grail story and gave it a Christian context for the first time.

After de Boron, a number of unknown writers (believed to have been Cistercian monks) created a series of linked romances, known as the *Vulgate Cycles* which incorporated the story of Lancelot and Gwenivere as a central element within Arthur's court. Previously this had been a separate story with Arthur almost incidental. With the production of the *Vulgate Cycles* the whole Arthurian story began to take on its accepted Christianised character. The decay which occurred in Arthur's court became due to the absence of Christian spiritual values amongst the Knights and Mordred is shown to be Arthur's incestuous son.

This *Vulgate Cycle* and the French poems became the accepted standard Arthurian works as the popularity of Arthur swept across Europe, spreading to Italy, Spain, Scandinavia and even Iceland. The Germans began writing their own versions - Ulrich Von Zatzikhoven wrote *'Lancelot'* in 1195 where Lancelot was brought up by the *'Lady of the Lake'* and Wolfram Von Eschenbach produced *'Percival'* which retold the Grail theme with the Grail being a magical stone rather than a vessel. Meanwhile, in England nothing new was added to the stories until much later when an unknown author produced 'Sir Gawain and the Green Knight' an adventure which took place around the setting of Arthur's court.

When Malory came to write his 'Morte de Arthur' he was able to draw on all the material mentioned, but in doing so he altered much of it. He left out a lot of the more supernatural-magic elements and people like Morgan-Le-Fay and Merlin were given much less prominence. In general, adventure and passion lost ground to romance and the Christian virtues. No doubt this is understandable as Malory was himself a Christian Knight who declared himself to be "....a true servant of Jesus". As one commentator, Eugene Vinaver points out his most cherished ideal was that of fidelity in marriage so obviously the extra-martial affair between Lancelot and Gwenivere formed the basis of his account of the downfall of Arthur's court. The fact that Arthur too was unfaithful and had an incestuous son (even though he was supposedly unaware of the incestuous nature of the liaison) puts the nail in the coffin as it were and Mordred was allowed to kill Arthur almost as an act of Divine punishment in the end.

Since Malory's version of events has become more or less standard it now seems normal to interpret Arthur's legend on the basis of the Christian religion with its accompanying morality and ethics of behaviour. As we mentioned before, however, this might not necessarily be the right interpretation because the stories did not always have a Christian emphasis. If we examine some of the earlier stories in more detail it is possible to see when and where changes were made which had a drastic effect on the character of the whole legend. We can see this process most clearly by looking at the Grail stories.

The first person to mention the Grail was the Frenchman Chrètein de Trôyes in his unfinished poem 'Perceval'. Here the hero, Perceval is raised by his mother in seclusion deep in the forest. Both his Father and elder brother were Knights who had died in combat and his mother did not wish the same to happen to him. When he came of age, however, Perceval was determined to become a Knight and he left home, breaking his mother's heart. After various adventures, including rescuing the maiden Blanchflor, he met a mysterious fisherman who offered him shelter in his castle. Within the castle were a large number of Knights and an old King who lay dying on a couch. Perceval was handed a sword with an inscription upon it and was told that he was meant to be its owner.

Before long a strange procession entered the hall. It was led by a Squire carrying a lance from the tip of which a constant stream of blood dripped. Two more Squires followed, each carrying candle sticks and then came a beautiful woman carrying a Grail vessel that shone so brightly that it made the candles seem dim. Finally, another woman carrying a silver serving dish brought up the rear. This strange procession passed through the hall three times but Perceval, who had been warned about his brashness in earlier adventures, decided not to ask any questions about it. The next morning when he awoke the castle was deserted. As he left, however, he met a very angry young woman who informed his that because he had failed to ask about the Grail the land was doomed to desolation. Later on in the poem Perceval learns that the old King was his uncle, the Fisher King, who had been wounded in the thigh by a spear. If he had asked the question "What is the Grail?" and "Whom does it serve?" the King would have been healed and the land would have been saved from desolation.

Another story about the Grail was written in the early part of the 13th Century by a German named Heinrich von dem Tûrlin. This story is called 'Diu Crône' and its hero is Gawain. A young Knight, Gawain, discovered a castle by accident. Inside an old King lay dying. A mysterious Grail procession took place as in the first story but this time the Grail and the other objects were all carried by women. In this version, Gawain actually asked about the Grail and the old King was miraculously restored to health. In another story which forms part of the *Vulgate Cycles*, Gawain is once again the hero. This time, however, he encountered twelve maidens in the Grail procession, all of whom were weeping for the Grail. Here he did not ask the question "Whom does it serve?" and the old King died.

By contrast to all this, Robert de Boron's Grail story, written in 1190, is quite different. In the other stories, the Grail is a mysterious object which sometimes seems to come and go of its own accord. It is an intensely beautiful object which has the ability to produce as much food and drink as the company can manage to consume but it remains an object of mystery and its nature is never really explained.

In De Boron's story the hero is once again Perceval but the Grail now becomes no less than the actual cup that Jesus used during the last supper, and the vessel in which Joseph of Arimathea (the man who buried Jesus) caught the last drops of Jesus's blood as he died on the cross.

De Boron maintains that Joseph brought this Holy relic to Britain and kept it in a secret place known as Avalon (a place long equated with Glastonbury in Somerset or Avon) where it was to be looked after by a series of special guardians known as the Grail Keepers.

By Arthur's time the exact whereabouts of the Grail were unknown. Anyone wishing to find it had to search for it. It was known, however, that the Grail Keeper or Fisher King lived in a mysterious castle surrounded by wasteland and water. The land had become wasted when the King was wounded but the land will revive and the King will be healed if a questor asks the right question. Again, the question being "Whom does it serve"?.

Robert de Boron, then, introduced a distinctly Christian version of the Grail theme. No longer a strange and mysterious vessel it now becomes a Holy Christian relic able to grant visions of Jesus and the Virgin Mary to those who are worthy, and it becomes a kind of symbol of special friendship between God and the Isles of Britain. This Christianised version of the Grail quest was subsequently developed by the writers of the *Vulgate Cycles* and by Malory to the point where only a questor who is 'pure' can obtain the Holy Grail.

The original all important question "Whom does it serve?" more or less lost its significance to the quest, and the really important thing seemed to be the ability to receive a kind of 'state of grace' from the Holy Grail itself and to be granted a vision.

By Malory's time the only one 'pure' enough to achieve the quest was Galahad. Gawain and Perceval were disregarded (presumably because they were associated with the pre-Christian Grail), Lancelot was too tainted by his affair with Gwenivere to be considered any longer, but Galahad, who is able to resist female temptation and was thus still 'pure', was rewarded by being allowed to fulfil his quest and blessed by being granted a vision of the Holy Grail.

This drastic change of emphasis in the nature of the Grail stories began then when Robert de Boron published his work in 1190 within just a few years of Chrètein de Trôyes poem (de Trôyes had died in 1188 leaving his 'Perceval' to be completed by an unidentified author).

Since it is generally safe to assume that new ideas, especially radical ones, do not suddenly appear out of thin air, the question arises what caused this change of emphasis? What prompted De Boron to take a story that was fast gaining in popularity and alter it so drastically by making an unknown, mysterious object into a Holy Christian relic and why was this particular theme chosen to be developed even more by subsequent writers? Part of the answer to these questions can undoubtedly be found in the strange events that took place in the year 1190 when de Boron was writing.

It was in this year of 1190 that the monks of Glastonbury Abbey caused a huge commotion when they exhumed a body from their churchyard and claimed it to be the body of King Arthur himself. They could not actually prove that it was Arthur but they made such a song and dance about it that even King Richard 'The Lion Heart', went to Glastonbury to inspect the remains for himself.

Now for a number of years before this event these monks had been trying to prove that Glastonbury was the oldest Christian site in England and furthermore, they claimed that Glastonbury was a much more important religious centre than a rival abbey in France. There is good reason to believe that it was these same monks who started the story about Joseph of Arimathea coming to Britain in the first place and founding a church on the site of their abbey.

If this were true then it would obviously make Glastonbury the oldest Christian church in the country and far more important than anything that France had to offer. To discover King Arthur's bones in the churchyard would undoubtedly have lent an air of credence to their claim since Arthur was taken away to Avalon to die and Avalon was associated with Joseph of Arimathea.

Unfortunately for the monks there was no actual proof that Joseph founded their abbey or that the exhumed body did in fact belong to Arthur. However, it was not long after this event that Robert de Boron produced his newly Christianised Grail story and his own story about Joseph of Arimathea. Quite obviously then there must be a connection between de Boron's stories and the machinations of the (mad?) monks, and since the exact identity of de Boron himself is unknown it is not totally out of the question that he was a monk himself.

The writers of the *Vulgate Cycles* who began to develop this theme of the 'Holy' Grail some thirty years after de Boron are suspected of being Cistercian monks because their stories are as much about Christian missionaries and other types of ecclesiasticals as they are about Arthur and his Knights.

Malory, as we have seen, was a self confessed servant of Jesus so he would obviously prefer the 'Holy' Grail version to that of the original and so then the Grail has passed into common acceptance as the Holy Grail, a wonderful, mysterious Christian relic. The fact remains, however, that there is no evidence whatsoever within Christian tradition to support the idea that the Grail has anything to do with Jesus.

The Grail is not recognised as a genuine holy relic by the Church. In fact the Church has remained strangely quiet about the whole affair. Surely if there were any evidence at all to back up this story it would have been the first institution to make as much capital out of it all as possible.

Nicholas Gold, in his book 'The Queen and the Cauldron', asks the question if the Grail had been a genuine holy relic would the Christian establishment ever have allowed it to be carried around by women even in a story? It hardly seems likely given their track record regarding women!

Back in 1913 a writer called Jessie Weston was questioning the Christian interpretation of the Grail stories and she pointed out that there is no ecclesiastical story to connect Joseph of Arimathea with the last supper and no evidence that he even came to Britain. She came to the conclusion that the Grail legend dates back to a pre-Christian religious tradition associated with the death and re-birth of the 'Nature God'.

Weston points out that the Grail stories that have Gawain as the hero seem to be older in origin than the other stories and in them the Grail procession is always accompanied by women or weeping women. There is always the presence of a dead or dying King and a land laid waste. There is also always the possibility of the King and the land being restored to health and vigour if the right question is asked about the Grail. The question being "Whom does it serve?" Furthermore, the King is always said to be 'wounded in the thigh' which is a medieval euphemism for 'wounded in the genitals'.

All this has a remarkable similarity to a pre-Christian religious tradition found at one time all over Europe and the Middle and Near East. This old religious tradition is associated with the worship of the Great Mother Goddess. More will be said about this religion in the following chapters but for the moment we will just consider certain aspects of it which are relevant to the understanding of the Grail stories.

The *Old Testament* of the *Bible* often mentions the Babylonian God known as Tammuz. He was the son or consort of the Goddess Ishtar. Tammuz died and was restored to life by Ishtar. The time of his death was a time of annual mourning and marked by a procession of women who invariably wept and wailed for him.

Similarly, the Greek God Adonis, consort or son of Aphrodite, was 'wounded in the thigh' by a wild boar and died. He was brought to the underworld and was restored to life by the Goddess of that realm, Persephone. Thereafter he spent half of the year with Aphrodite and half with Persephone. Every Autumn his departure to the underworld was always marked by the women who wept and mourned for him.

The story of the Goddess Cybele and her lover, Attis, was another example of this so called 'death and re-birth' cycle. Here Attis was driven mad by Cybele after he was unfaithful to her. In his madness he castrated himself and bled to death. After a while the Goddess relented and restored him to life. His death was also mourned annually and there was always a great procession which passed through the streets.

Now this ancient religious tradition of the death and re-birth of the son or consort of a powerful Goddess is to be found all over the Middle East and Europe. It is part of what Christian scholars and historians like to call a 'fertility-cult'. Here the vitality of the land and the destiny of the people who depend upon the land is in turn dependant upon the health and vigour of the King or Goddess consort. It the King is old or ill the land is said to suffer; it becomes wasted and unproductive. The women mourn the loss of the King and the crops. If the King is healed, or the consort resurrected, then the land is also restored. The parallels that can be drawn between these old religious traditions and the events that take place within the Grail stories are immediately obvious. The dying King or consort, often 'wounded in the thigh', the mysterious processions, the wasted land that is restored if the King is restored to health. The two are undoubtedly connected. Weston suggests then, that the Grail stories have far more in common with the old religion of the Mother Goddess than they could possibly have with Christianity.

In order to answer these questions it is necessary to look a little more closely at the origins of the Grail stories themselves.

Chapter Two

As we saw in the last chapter, the religious significance of the Grail stories is far more likely to be non-Christian than Christian. It echoes loudly a religious tradition that goes back long before Christianity was thought of. We also know from the previous chapter that the earliest written form of the Grail story was written by Chrètein de Trôyes in about 1188 while the earliest Christianised form was by de Boron some two or three years later. However, Heinrich von Turlin's *'Diu Krone'*, although written some years later, contains a lot of material which appears to be very much earlier in origin than either of them. There is good reason to believe that this version is based largely upon stories told by a Welsh bard known as Bleheris or Blihis who died some twenty-five years before Chrètein de Trôyes began his work.

In Bleheris's account the hero, Gawain, rides through a land laid waste and comes by chance on a mysterious castle close to the sea. Inside the castle is the body of a dead Knight. Gawain witnesses a mysterious Grail procession and also sees a lance fixed upright in a silver cup. From its tip flows a continuous stream of blood.

Gawain asks about the lance but not about the Grail and when he awakens the next morning the castle is gone.

The land around him, however, has been partially restored. Fresh water is flowing once more. As he leaves he meets a woman who is angry with him for not asking about the Grail as well for if he had asked about it the land would have been fully restored along with the King.

This account, although not directly connected to Arthur, seems to be the earliest form of the Grail story. It comes from Wales, a country with a long Celtic tradition and seems to have been taken across to France by the Welsh bards or storytellers, probably first to Brittany which also has a strong Celtic heritage. If the stories originated in Wales it seems highly likely that they formed part of the much larger Celtic tradition. A substantial amount of Irish and Welsh folklore has been preserved in written form and it is possible to compare this with the Grail stories in order to see if there are indeed common elements and connections.

First of all in the Grail stories a number of magical objects are mentioned, a broken sword with an inscription upon it, a spear that bleeds and the Grail itself which seems to be some kind of vessel in most stories, except for Van Eschenbach's account where the Grail is a stone.

The word 'Grail' is actually a French word meaning a deep serving dish rather than a cup or vessel and in the early stories the Grail is able to mysteriously supply unlimited amounts of food and drink for the guests at the castle. Now amongst the most prized possessions of the average Celtic household was its cauldron or large metal pot used for cooking purposes.

The gift of a cauldron was a mark of great esteem and indeed the Celts turned cauldron making into a fine art. Archaeologists have discovered many beautifully decorated cauldrons surviving from the Celtic times such as the famous Gundestrop cauldron found preserved in a Danish peat bog. Obviously there is a similarity here between the Celtic cauldron and the Grail object. Cauldrons were not only used for cooking and serving food they were objects also of beauty and value in their own right. The Grail was not only a very beautiful object but it also had the capability of supplying food and drink.

In Celtic folklore there are numerous stories to be found concerning magic cauldrons. In the Welsh poem "*Culhwch and Olwen*" there is actually a quest theme concerning magic cauldrons.

King Arthur himself led a quest to the underworld at the request of his cousin Culhwch. Culhwch wanted to marry Olwen but her father refused consent unless Culhwch was able to obtain certain objects, amongst which were four magical cauldrons which would automatically produce a constant supply of food and drink for the guests of the wedding feast.

In another story, Bran the Blessed, a giant who ruled the Isle of the Mighty (Britain), also had a magical cauldron which came from a lake in Ireland. This cauldron could bring slain warriors back to life and no-one went away from it unsatisfied.

An even earlier Celtic story also featured a magical cauldron. It is about the Dagda or Good God of the Tuatha De Danann (people of the Goddess Danu), who, when he first arrived in Ireland, brought with him a magical cauldron that could feed everyone. He not only brought his cauldron with him, however, he also brought the spear of Lug, which guaranteed victory to its owner; the sword of Nuadu, from which no-one could escape, and a magical stone, the Great Fal or Stone of Destiny, which shrieked when a future King stood upon it. This same magical stone was said to have been taken to Scotland when it became known as the stone of Scone. Edward 1 had it removed from Scotland and built it into the coronation chair in Westminster Abbey, presumably to make sure that the two Kingdoms of Scotland and England would have only one King from that time onwards.

All this cannot be mere co-incidence. The earliest Grail stories can be traced back to Celtic Wales and the mysterious objects within the tales are easily identifiable as having special significance within Celtic Legend. It seems rather obvious then that these facts, combined with the complete lack of evidence to support the claim that the Grail is (or ever was) a Christian relic, point to the Grail stories being Celtic in origin rather than Christian. Furthermore, if, as Weston suggested, there are easily identifiable non-Christian religious aspects of the stories as well then what we actually have in the Grail stories is Celtic tradition set in a non-Christian religious background.

If we take some time to consider in more detail this underlying Celtic/religious background aspect we will be in a better position to understand exactly how it may have influenced the actions of Arthur and his court. That is, how it may have influenced both the real Arthur of history and the Arthur of the legend. More than this it will help to explain events which take place within the legend itself - events which until now have either remained shrouded in mystery or have been given a thin veneer of Christian explanation which hardly does them justice at all. Furthermore it will also help to shed new light on the motives of the characters involved in the stories. To begin with we need to examine the religion that the Celts practised.

The bias of Christianity over the years has almost succeeded in convincing us that the religion practised by the Celts was merely 'Paganism'. This is generally taken to mean a kind of idol or nature worshipping cult vastly inferior to the so-called higher religions. In years gone by Christians also held this attitude towards religions such as Islam or Buddhism but lately they are inclined to treat some rival religions with a little more respect, presumably because of the vast numbers of people now practising alternative religions especially Islam, the world-wide membership of which now equals, if not outnumbers, those claiming to be Christians. Islam is currently a very powerful religious movement and thus historians and the like have to be far more careful in their criticisms.

This same caution does not apply to the age old religion of the Celts. It is still acceptable common practice to dismiss it as a series of Pagan cults. Thus people like Geoffrey Ashe and others constantly refer to the 'cult' of the Mother Goddess or the 'cult' of this Goddess and the 'cult' of that Goddess, or even more dismissively, describe it as a mere 'fertility-cult'. This way of referring to the old Celtic religion serves to give the impression that it was an unimportant, unorganised, fragmented affair with one Goddess worshipped here and another Goddess worshipped there. It gives the impression too that there were many Gods and Goddesses all different and that the worship of each one represented a different fertility cult -

or different brand of idolatry. It has been described as having a Pantheon of different Deities with a different God or Goddess for every tribe and one for each different aspect of life, such as Gods for war, Gods for the corn, Goddesses of childbirth and so on.

The truth is that the Celts practised the ancient religion of the Great Mother Goddess. This is a religion that came into being at the very dawn of humanity and is based upon the principle that the ultimate being who created the world and the universe is female. This religion has been greatly maligned and misrepresented ever since a rival religion was started which claimed that the ultimate source of creation was male not female. The Mother Goddess religion started off in a very simple uncomplicated manner (as indeed did people themselves) and developed into a world-wide religion that knew no equal or rival until roughly around 2,400 BC.

The earliest archaeological evidence about the history of religion demonstrates beyond any shadow of doubt that our early predecessors regarded the Creative force of the universe as female rather than male. All over the known world our ancestors fashioned out of bone, wood and clay small statuettes which conveyed the concept of the female creative power. These statuettes, commonly called Venus figures by historians, have been found in all the areas that were known to have been inhabited since the earliest times. From the Middle East, through Southern Europe, Central and Eastern Europe right through to Siberia. Often they would be discovered in specially carved out niches in rocks or within primitive wall structures. The earliest of these statuettes have been dated at around 25,000 BC and they were produced right up until about 6,000 BC.

It is, of course, impossible to know exactly what these early people thought and exactly how they worshipped but amongst archaeologists there is now a fair consensus of opinion that these statuettes represent the earliest versions of the Mother Goddess religion.

Many historians have remarked upon the similarity that the figures have to the statues which have been found in temples dated at a much later time which were known to have been dedicated to the Mother Goddess, leading them to the conclusion that the 'Venus' figurines represented the early unsophisticated religious beliefs of our ancestors. Using the term 'unsophisticated' here is not meant to imply that this was in any way an inferior kind of religious worship. It is simply an indication that in these very early times, people had not progressed to the trappings and finery that we associate with religion today. They had no St Paul's Cathedral or Mecca, they left no traces of a grand religious hierarchy such as we find nowadays in Roman Catholicism. They simply seem to have experienced the creative force as female and regarded Her as the Great Mother.

In all the archaeological investigations that have been made over the inhabited sites covering 25,000 BC to 6,000 BC there have been no corresponding finds of male statuettes. There is no archaeological evidence to support the notion that our ancestors believed in God the Father. This idea did not enter into our history until about 2,400 BC. We therefore have an immense period of time in the history of the human race when people worshipped only the Great Mother. For roughly 22,500 years this was the one and only religion!

At first this religion was, as already mentioned, an unsophisticated affair but slowly as the human population itself became more sophisticated so did its religion. People discovered agriculture, they began living in settled communities around regions of fertile land. The Middle East was the birthplace of civilisation and here small villages grew into thriving urban centres. By 7,000 BC in Jericho (Cannan) for example, people were living in plastered brick houses with chimneys and doors, and everywhere there were shrines to the Mother Goddess containing the familiar statuettes.

Professor H.W. Saggs comments that the Mother Goddess represented by such figurines seems to have been the central figure in Neolithic religion. One community of about 2,000 people which was excavated in Anatolia Turkey revealed no less than 40 shrines dedicated to the Mother Goddess.

The invention of writing around 3,000 BC allowed historians to make far more accurate observations about early life and culture. They have discovered abundant evidence throughout the Near and Middle East that people worshipped the Mother Goddess. The religion by now was more organised with specially built temples administered by full time Priestesses and Priests. Gradually as civilisation spread across to the European Continent so did this more sophisticated form of the religion and temples to the Goddess were to be found in all major urban centres around the Mediterranean.

Britain at this time, however, was neither urban nor heavily populated. One estimate puts its population at a mere 10,000 people by the year 8,000 BC. There was, over the centuries, a very gradual influx of people from the

European Continent and by about 5,000 BC they had introduced plant civilisation and animal rearing. These people were the early Celts and their religion was the unsophisticated type of Goddess worship that had prevailed in the Middle East before urbanisation began. As noted before, the familiar 'Venus' statues have been found all over Europe including Britain. Indeed, one such figure found at the bottom of an abandoned British flint mine, was dated as late as 2,500 BC.

These early Celts worshipped in sacred groves of trees, and at wells; they constructed special square enclosures and everywhere erected the familiar standing stone circles and megaliths of which over 900 still exist today in Britain alone.

The most famous stone circle is of course Stonehenge, constructed at about 2,700 BC. These circles and megaliths were tribal focal points and shrines as well as places of burial and formed part of the religious life of the early Celts. As noted by historians Lloyd and Jennifer Lang, between the stone circle builders and the Druids there were no major waves of immigrants into the British Isles so it is possible to claim with some certainty that Stonehenge was indeed built by Bronze Age 'Druids'.

This all gives a clear indication that the religion of the Celts developed originally from the same spontaneous feeling of awe and reverence towards the Female Creative principle that all early human beings seem to have shared. It was not a series of strange cults developed in isolation from the rest of humanity as was once so casually assumed or inferred by so many historians. Some scholars at least are now beginning to realise that it was part of the same religious network that covered the rest of the world at that time. For instance the Langs themselves suggest that there is growing evidence that the Celtic religion of the Druids developed from something much older, something which was part of prehistoric European belief.

There is also no reason to believe that Britain was an isolated country cut off from the rest of the world. Even as far back as 4,000 BC there is evidence of trade between Britain and the European Continent with the early Britons exporting pottery and the stone axes. By about 1,500 BC trading was commonplace even with Mediterranean lands so it is not hard to imagine that similar religious traditions would have evolved even in different countries (or territories) especially when the Great Mother was a common focal point for worship. These early traders would have seen the great temples built in honour of the Mother Goddess. They may even have worshipped in them and they would certainly have told everyone all about them when they arrived back home.

By 3,000 BC then the major religion of the world was that of the Great Mother Goddess. This was a religion common to all those that we know anything about including those early Celts who were the ancestors of King Arthur. For thousands of years the Goddess was worshipped on Her own as the Mother of Creation and then at some point, exactly when is not known, a male Deity began to be introduced into Her religion. This male Deity usually appears as Her son who was also Her consort or lover. He was a young-God and the Goddess always had precedence over him. Throughout the religion of the Great Mother the son or young-God remained by Her side but always as a far less powerless figure. It was this God who came to represent the passing of the seasons, the growth of the crops and the eternal cycle of birth, death and renewal. The Goddess never died but the young-God was born, grew to maturity, died and was resurrected by the Goddess.

Time and time again this cycle of events was expressed in the religious practices of the Goddess worshipping peoples in many different countries through many different centuries. Damuzi was the consort of Inanna, of Sumer, he died because he became arrogant towards the Goddess and was sent to the underworld by Her (is this perhaps where the word "damned" came from with its connotation of being sent to hell?).

Tammuz was the son/consort of Ishtar (Babylon in Mesopotamia, 18th - 6th Century BC). Tammuz died accidentally while still quite young and Ishtar mourned his death. Attis was the lover of Cybele. He was driven mad by Her after he took another lover. In his madness he castrated himself and bled to death. Adonis was the son/lover of Aphrodite, Osiris the son/lover of Isis.

All these young Gods or Consorts died and were mourned as an integral part of the religious life of each year. In the Autumn or Winter their death was mourned, in the Spring their birth or resurrection was rejoiced in. Always the Mother Goddess remained while the son/consort died.

This annual death and rebirth is perhaps one of the major aspects of the Mother Goddess religion which bridges vast expanses both geographically and chronologically.

It was a recurrent theme right from the earliest literature of Sumer (3,000 BC) to Roman times and it was known and celebrated by the Celts. Here lies the real significance of the Grail stories. They are thinly disguised accounts of one of the central aspects of the Mother Goddess religion as practised by the Celts. The dying King represents the young-God or Consort of the Goddess. The state of the land, whether it is fruitful and productive or whether it is wasted or barren, is synonymous with the health of the King. If the King is reborn or resurrected then the land will no longer be wasted.

Jessie West spotted the resemblance of the Grail stories to elements within the Middle Eastern and Mediterranean versions of the Goddess religion or 'mystery religions' of the East as she called them. She did not identify the link between this religion and the religion that the Celts practised, however, neither did she examine the link between the Celtic tradition and the Grail stories.

The sons/Consorts of the Celtic Mother Goddesses are not so well known as their Mediterranean or Middle Eastern counterparts. These ancient Celts were never interested in writing things down for posterity. They never left any manuscripts or texts behind, instead they preferred to commit their traditions and knowledge to the memory of the storytellers or bards who recounted events and histories with such skill that it could be considered an art form in itself. Bleheris of Wales was such a storyteller. It was from material provided by him that the first Grail stories were written.

The story of the Grail is no less than the French version of a Welsh tale telling traditions of a religion that had apparently vanished off the face of the Earth some 600 years before.

What a remarkable testimony to the art of Celtic storytelling to keep it alive for so long! No doubt if this had been written down before in a more readily understandable form it would probably never have survived at all. The Christians would have destroyed both manuscript and author very quickly. As it was Chrètien de Trôyes himself died in somewhat mysterious circumstances, in a fire, before he could finish his own version of the Grail which was then (surprise-surprise) conveniently finished off for him by a Christian monk. Two years later came de Boron and his 'Holy' Grail version, which soon became accepted as the standard interpretation.

As we have shown, however, it is much more likely that the religious significance of the Grail story is pre-Christian and moreover, non-Christian which was one very good reason for the Christian establishment to try and alter its interpretation as soon as possible. We suggest that the Grail story was recognised by the Church for what it was - a symbol or echo of the Mother Goddess religion that had been in existence long before Christianity and which was still a potential rival to it.

Since the stories of Arthur and the tales about the Grail were so immensely popular it would have been important to the Church to Christianise them as soon as possible before others recognised the content of the stories and perhaps attempted to revive the Old Religion once more.

Chapter Three

To the Celts the Goddess was known by many different names such as Brigit (from whom the name of Britain is derived), the Morrigan, Tara, Tlachtga, Medb, Coventina, Sulis and Danu to name but a few. Similarly, the young-God or Consort was known as the Green Man, Belenos, Cernunnos, Herne, the Dagda, Lugh and the Oak King.

There were times of special worship such as Samhain in November, Beltain in May, Lughnassa in August. These were occasions when the gathering of the harvest or the rebirth of the young-God was celebrated. In times of trouble, such as war or crop failure, an image of the Goddess might be carried around in procession so that people could receive a special blessing (in much the same way that an image of the Virgin Mary is often used in Catholic processions today).

When Christianity came to Britain this Old Religion was its main rival just as it was or had been in other parts of the world. When the Romans invaded they attacked and defeated the Druid order (as explained in the Introduction), but they did not attempt to suppress the

religion itself. This is because they were in fact very familiar with it.

The Mother Goddess religion was widely practised in Rome and Greece and had been so for many many centuries before. They recognised the Celtic version of the religion as a variation of their own religion so they built smart new temples to the Goddess and simply added their own Roman names to them.

At Bath, for instance, where the Goddess Sulis was revered by the locals a new temple was built and dedicated to Minerva. Both Sulis and Minerva had long associations with healing and water so they were worshipped under the same name. There was no destruction involved, just a simple name change.

A similar thing happened at Buxton Spa and as historian Anne Ross explains in her book on the 'Everyday life of the Pagan Celts', the baths are decorated with both Roman and native British images but it feels like the Roman representations only exist to give more tangible form to the native beliefs which caused the sacred springs to be dedicated to Sulis in the first place. Clearly, then, the early Romans were reasonably at ease with the Celtic ways of worship.

To the Christians, however, the Old Religion was very much a threat. It undermined the very basis of their belief in a supreme male God. When the Roman Emperors converted to Christianity they began to suppress Goddess worship wherever they could. Temple after temple throughout Europe was closed and destroyed. The old worship was forbidden wherever they were powerful enough to do so. In Britain by this time though, the

Roman Empire was beginning to lose its grip and Christianity, still in its infancy, was not strong enough on its own to simply force a change on the population. It had to resort to other tactics.

When the Romans suddenly left, the old religion, as we saw in the Introduction, was still very much alive and the old traditions were quickly being re-established as the Celts prepared themselves to fight for their survival against the power of the invading Saxons. Without an adequate power base, Christianity could not hope to crush its more popular rival.

The first problem facing the newly established Christian community then was to encourage as many people as possible to join their faith so that they could work from a position of power. Once this was achieved (and it took several centuries), they were in a better position to attack the old religion more effectively and suppress it so that it no longer presented a threat. Now the manner in which it was able to achieve this initial edge over the Goddess Religion is of major importance to our consideration of the legend of King Arthur and will be discussed at some length later in the chapter.

Suffice it so say for the moment that Christianity was able to offer the male sex in particular a new perspective on life. A perspective which had immediate appeal for a great many men and which allowed Christianity to make converts fairly quickly.

Firstly, though, we would like to consider a few of the many ways in which Christianity was later able to suppress the old religion and keep it suppressed once it had achieved its power base amongst the population. Now aside from the obvious coercive tactics which were used, such as passing laws to make sure everyone attended church on Sunday (and of course the use or threat of brute force if they refused) one of the least subtle of its ploys was simply to try and persuade people that the ways and traditions of the old religion were actually evil. For example, one representation of the Goddess Consort, Cernunnos, was particularly popular with the Celts and as a symbol of his link with nature and the forest animals he was quite often depicted with horns. So too was Herne the Hunter, another popular form of the young-God. By medieval times this representation of the young-God was being openly abused by the Christians as a symbol of evil. They clearly began to equate him with the devil of their own scriptures, something they would not have dared to do centuries before.

As Ross points out, in later Christian illustrated manuscripts Cernunnos had clearly become symbolic of the devil and anti-Christian forces in general which gives a good indication of how important he was to the Celtic religion if they felt it was necessary to malign him in such a manner.

For thousands and thousands of years the young-God (whatever his name at the time) had been loved, respected, looked up to and admired by countless generations of people. He had been their symbol of all that was good in nature and in life. It was his sacrifice that ensured their prosperity. His death and re-birth made certain that the land on which everyone depended was not a wasteland.

Now some 500 or 600 years after the last Goddess temple was forced to close down the young-God was transformed by the Christians into an evil being. This was, without doubt, a piece of pure propaganda which still seems to have an effect even today.

A later device employed by Christianity and its supporters was infinitely more subtle and possibly even more effective in damaging the credibility of the Old Mother Goddess religion. Like the tactics mentioned above, it has also proved useful right up until this present time. This was the device of pretending that the old religion did not actually exist. It was denied its true status as a religion. If mentioned at all it was (and still is) dismissed as nothing more than a 'Fertility Cult' or as a branch of primitive pagan idolatry. It was the cult of a particular goddess here or a particular 'nature' god there and always written as 'goddess' with a small 'g', never with a capital letter as if to impress the notion that this was really a being and a religion of little importance. When something like this is reiterated over and over again, people tend to believe it without any questions asked, especially when the writer is considered to be an 'expert' on the subject.

In fact, far from being genuine scientific observers of history who simply note down the facts that have been discovered, most archaeologists and historians exhibit an extraordinary amount of unscientific Christian bias which completely colours the nature of their work.

For example, as Merlin Stone points out, the worship of a female deity has for the most part been included as a minor addition to the study of the patterns of religions beliefs in ancient cultures, and in so many books a cursory mention of the Goddess often precedes lengthy dissertations about the male deities who replaced Her. She goes on to say that especially misleading are the numerous vague inferences that the veneration of a female deity was a separate, unusual or curious occurrence.

Since the Mother Goddess has been worshipped in one form or another from about 25,000 BC it can scarcely be regarded as a minor or unusual occurrence. It was in reality a massive religion, the true scope of which is hard for us to appreciate now after so many centuries of deliberate misinformation.

Stone maintains that it is difficult to grasp the immensity and significance of the extreme reverence paid to this Goddess over a period of either twenty-five thousand years (as the Upper Palaeolithic evidence suggests), or even seven thousand years (as written records show) and over miles of land, cutting across national boundaries and vast expanses of sea. Yet we must do just that in order to fully comprehend the longevity as well as the widespread power and influence this religion once held.

Some readers might take offence at the notion of historians and archaeologists being biased individuals who have been mis-leading the public for years. Could it be that these eminent scholars are simply unable to recognise that the worship of a mother Goddess could be a real religion? Perhaps they have been confused by the fact that the Goddess was known by so many different names. For example, in early Sumeria the Goddess was known by names such as Nina, Nanshe, Innana, in Egypt she was Hathor or Isis, in Crete it was Aphrodite, in Rome she was Cybele, Hera, Diana, in Britain Cerridwen, Brigit and so on. However, if we stop to consider for a moment (as good historians should) is it really that surprising that the Goddess was called by so many different names? We are after all talking about regions covering many thousands of miles in an age when any communication between even neighbouring villages must have been sporadic and unusual compared to the ease and efficiency which we communicate with one another today.

There were very few people who could read or write and in any case clay and stone tablets would not have been delivered around like morning papers. There were no radios, televisions or telephones. The modern tendency towards standardisation was a long way into the future. Society was just developing so it is really not surprising that there were countless local variations.

We also have an enormous time scale to take into consideration. Looking at just the historical period from about 5,000 BC to 500 AD (when the last Goddess temples were closed down), we have a period of some 5,500 years development. Names and customs were bound to change over such a length of time.

Consider how the English language has changed in a mere 500 years. People using modern English would have a great deal of difficulty understanding medieval speech if time travel were possible. Reading medieval script is difficulty enough. In fact it is really quite remarkable that through all these different regions with their unique customs and languages and over such an enormous length of time, the Goddess religion has remained as a constant identifiable factor throughout.

How scholars and historians have failed to recognise this common underlying religious direction is also quite remarkable. It is as if some historian or sociologist of the year 3,000 AD were to look back at the religions of this century and conclude that the people who inhabited the area of Britain then known as Wales, belonged to a Baptist cult while those around Manchester belonged to a Protestant Ethic cult and those in London worshipped a deity called St Paul, whose chief prophet was called Christopher Wren.

If scholars can so easily conclude that the worship of Astarte as the Great Mother is totally different from the worship of Isis as the Great Mother and different again from the worship of Cybele, Brigit or Cerridwen as the Great Mother, then presumably they would also be unable to see any connection at all between Roman Catholicism, the Church of England and the Church of the Later Day Saints, or even the Sunni Moslems and the Sheite Moslems.

Regardless of differences which might occur in styles of worship or as the result of theological nit-picking, it is not normal to assume that these sub-groups do not form part of a specific religion. Modern differences are not explained away as the 'cult' of the Jehovah's Witnesses or the 'cult' of the Virgin Mary. Both are recognised as different developments within the basic religion of Christianity. Why then do scholars persist in describing the religion of the Great Mother as if it were just a series of different cults unrelated to one another? There can only be two answers to this question. Either historians and religious scholars are so lacking in intelligence and imagination that they are genuinely unable to see the basic connection, or they are reluctant to admit that the connections exist because of extreme bias. Since in most other respects these scholars and historians seem perfectly intelligent and able people, we must conclude that bias is the main source of the problem.

If it is in fact the case that prejudice against the Mother Goddess religion still exists amongst scholars even today, we have to ask ourselves the question why? Why should anyone be that concerned about a religion which for all intents and purposes vanished from the face of the earth about 1,500 years ago? Part of the answer undoubtedly lies in the fact that, for some at least, the bias is now unconscious.

The Christian establishment has done such a good job in convincing society at large that the Mother Goddess religion was an inferior or even evil cult that the validity of this idea now goes unchallenged by historians and scholars alike. In fact they have accepted this point of view so completely that they do not even notice that they are sharing it.

The others who are aware of what they are doing probably realise that the old religion is not quite dead even now. For here and there, throughout the British Isles traces still remain. Public houses called The Green Man are far from uncommon. Old traditions such as 'Well Dressing' (a celebration to the Goddess in Spring time at the site of Her holy wells), Maypole dancing, stag-dances, hobby horse processions, Morris dancing and many more local customs have survived the ages.

Carved into hillsides around the South and West of Britain are numerous huge white horses. Thousands of years old, these beautiful figures represented the Goddess and on a hillside in Dorset stands the enormous Cerne Abbas giant - a representation of the young-God.

These and many other similar figures are still looked after and respected by the local people even today. All of these things are echo's of the old religion. Links with our Celtic past, alive and kicking in the 20th Century.

Now it may seem to the average reader at this point that we have digressed a long way away from the study of King Arthur and his legend which is, after all, what this book is meant to be about. Please bear with us a little longer for what we are about to discuss now has a crucial bearing on the understanding of the whole story.

As far as Arthur and his court are concerned, one of the most important aspects of the old Mother Goddess religion is the status it gave to women and the effect that this had on society in general. As one might expect, in a society where a female divinity was held in supreme reverence rather than a male divinity, women were accorded a tremendous amount of respect.

Historical evidence shows clearly that in these kinds of societies women were not considered to be the inferior sex. They owned their own businesses, they could choose who they wished to have as a husband and they could also obtain a divorce fairly easily if they wanted to. For example, in early Sumer (now Southern Iraq) Professor Saggs concluded that between 3,000 BC - 1800 BC women were much better off than they subsequently became. They ran the temples, owned property, lent money and were the official scribes, (incidentally, the earliest discovered examples of writing dated 3,200 BC were found in the temple of the Goddess Inanna and were records of the temple accounts).

The women were often regarded as the heads of the family and were the main breadwinners. Herodotus of Greece wrote about Egypt where "women go in the market place, transact affairs and occupy themselves with business while their husbands stay home".

In fact, in these societies where the Goddess was worshipped as the supreme divinity, maternity rather than paternity was the all important principle. Children were described as the offspring of their mothers rather than of their fathers. Inheritance ran through the female side of the family rather than the male line, going from mother to daughter, instead of father to son. This kind of social organisation is called Matrilineal and within such matrilineal cultures not only names but possessions, titles and territorial rights are inherited through the female line. (In some parts of Africa, Indonesia and Micronesia this custom still exists today).

For example, the well known anthropologist, Margaret Mead, demonstrated that the Royal House of Egypt was Matrilineal for most of its long existence. Tracing back the lineage of the Royal Family she discovered that it was the daughters of the household who actually inherited the throne rather than the sons. (The Goddess Isis, as a symbol no doubt of this female sovereignty, was often referred to as 'The Throne'). A man only became King in Egypt by marrying the Royal princess who was next in line for the title of Queen. Mead suggests that this is probably the reason why, much later on in the history of Egypt, the custom of marrying brother with sister developed because that was the only way the son of the Royal household could ever hope to become King. It was only from the time of the 18th Dynasty (1570 - 1300 BC) that the term 'Pharaoh' was being used to signify the important Royal male of the household.

Another example of the custom of matrilineal inheritance was reported by the Greek historian, Diodorus, after he travelled through Anatolia (modern day Turkey). Here the laws were established by the Queen and the rights of the throne belonged to the Queen's daughter and succeeding women in the family line.

Another historian, Charles Seltman, writing about Crete states that a man became King or Chieftain only by a formal marriage and his daughter, not his son, succeeded so that the next Chieftain was the youth who married his daughter.

It is precisely this practise of matrilineal inheritance that is all important to our consideration of King Arthur because there is ample evidence to demonstrate that the Goddess worshipping Celts also inherited titles and property through the female line rather than the male line. Under the laws of matrilineal succession, the new King was not the son of the old King but the new Queen was the daughter of the old Queen. The man who married the new Queen became the new King. It was the Queen who represented the line of sovereignty. This was true of the Goddess worshipping lands of the Middle East and the Mediterranean and it was also true of the British Celts. If Arthur was a Celt, which he undoubtedly was, and if he followed the old Celtic traditions then the way in which he could become King would be greatly affected. The fact that he was the son of a King himself would not automatically mean that he would become one too. In order to become a King, he like anyone else, would have to marry the Queen who held sovereignty over some particular territory.

Matrilineal succession was normal Celtic practise. Consider the old Irish tale of Niall and the nine hostages. Niall was the youngest of five sons who were looking for water while out hunting. They came upon a well but it was owned by an old hag who would only allow water to be drawn from it on condition that each of the brothers gave her a kiss. She was so loathsome looking that they all declined the offer except Niall who kissed her. Instantly she changed into a beautiful woman and said that her name was Flaithius or Sovereignty and that Niall would now become King of all Ireland.

Consider too, the *Anglo Saxon Chronicles* compiled around 890 AD. Referring to the Picts ".....and they asked the Scots for wives and they were given them on condition that they always chose their Royal race in the female line and they observed this for a long time afterwards".

It was a long standing Celtic practise to be named after one's mother, which is a sure sign of matrilineal inheritance. For instance, in the famous Irish story of *'The Cattle Raid of Cooley'* the hero Conchobar is brought up by his father, Cathbad, but is known as 'Conchobar mac Nessa', or son of Nes (his mother) rather than 'mac Cathbad'. His mother Nes married Fergus mac Roich (Roich is Fergus's mother not his father), the God Lug is known as 'Lug mac Ethnenn' (Ethnenn being a female name) and so on.

Another indication of the practise of matrilineal succession is to be found within the old folk or fairy tales such as those collected by the brothers Grimm. So many of these stories tell of ordinary men or youths who manage to become Kings by marrying a King's daughter. If the Royal inheritance had passed to the King's son (as would be the case today), then these adventurer/hero's would simply have become the new King's brother-in-law. Since, however, they actually became Kings themselves, these stories are demonstrations of the custom of matrilineal succession - a folk memory of the way things were "Once upon a time".

Indeed Nicholas Gold maintains that in the original versions, before they were "cleaned up" through centuries of Christian influence, it was more a case of the Queen's husband being replaced by a younger and more able King.

In the Welsh tale of Culwch and Olwen, Olwen's father, Ysbaddaden, is described in some versions as Olwen's husband rather than her father. This would explain his reluctance at the idea of Culwch actually marrying Olwen because then Culwch would become King and he himself would be redundant. Indeed, in the story after Culwch does eventually marry Olwen he has Ysbaddaden killed. This story is a reflection of a custom which developed alongside the practise of matrilineal succession. It concerns the replacement of the old King by a younger and healthier successor and this too had its beginnings in the old Mother Goddess religion. As we noted earlier, the Great Mother has a son or Consort who invariably dies and is resurrected and this was celebrated annually as part of the religious calendar.

A custom developed whereby the High Priestess was taken to represent the Goddess. The King or Ruler of the region was the man who married the High Priestess and he represented the young-God or Consort of the Goddess. It was the High Priestess who conferred Kingship in these early civilisations and amongst the Celts it was the Queen who represented the Goddess and conferred Kingship.

Evidence seems to suggest that in most places the Queen and the high Priestess were generally the same person in much the same way that the head of the British Royal family is also automatically the head of the Church of England. The twin roles of High Priestess and Queen are repeatedly referred to in tablets and texts from early historic times in the Near East. For instance, the director of the Archaeological Museum at Iraklion has stated that the alabaster throne at Knossos was intended for the Priestess or Queen who personified the Goddess, and Ross and Robins discuss the likelihood of Boudicca of the Iceni tribe being both Queen and High Priestess at the same time.

If the Consort of the Priestess-Queen was taken to represent the young-God and the young-God was associated with the fertility of the land (an essential concern in those early agricultural societies), then the Consort or King presumably needed to be young and healthy in order to fulfil his symbolic role. Presumably, likwise, he was replaced by a younger, fitter model every so often.

This, of course, brings us squarely back to the significance of the Grail story which can now be understood as a symbolic enactment of the replacement of the old dying or infertile King with the new prospective candidate, namely, the questing Knight. It is interesting to note that in all of the early non-Christian Grail stories the young Knight had an amorous encounter with at least one maiden before he came upon the Grail castle and its strange inhabitants, as if to verify the young man's sexual ability before he assumed the position of new King. In the Christianised versions of the Grail story, however, (especially in the more developed version by Malory), the Grail candidate was not tested in this way. Indeed the sexual nature of the Grail quest was totally denied because only a Knight who was 'pure' i.e., one who had no previous sexual experience, was able/allowed to obtain the Grail vision.

The idea of a younger, healthier King replacing the old King as a symbolic gesture to the death and re-birth of the young-God seems to have been started by the Queens/Priestesses of the Middle East. They invariably chose annual Consorts rather than permanent husbands, with the old Consort returning to 'civilian' life after the year of his reign. In some cases, however, it appears that the old King may actually have been killed (perhaps for refusing to be made redundant!), or, as later documents show, rituals were enacted where an effigy or animal sacrifice was substituted for the King instead. In other cases the King seems to have been re-appointed annually for further terms of office after a ceremony where he would receive a ritual blow or some other such symbolic gesture meant to represent the death and re-birth of the young-God.

Whichever was the case in any particular country, one thing was certain, and this is very important. There was no Divine right of permanent Kingship under the religion of the Mother Goddess. The fact that the Goddess ruled eternally while the young-God or Consort died and was resurrected by Her was designed to demonstrate that the male did not necessarily have preference over the female.

No man was automatically King for life just because his father was King. If a man aspired to be King or leader he had first to be chosen by the Queen/Priestess. It was more a position of merit than birthright. This practise at least made sure that the leadership of the community was chosen from amongst the best on offer and its subjects were not condemned to be ruled automatically by the son of the old King. In times of war a good proven warrior could be chosen, in times of peace, someone with other skills such as agricultural knowledge, political diplomacy or whatever was needed by the community at that particular time could be chosen.

It is not necessarily the case that the son of a good King always turns out to be a good King himself. He could be half-witted, he could be a blood-thirsty tyrant forever dragging the Kingdom into unnecessary wars, or he could be simply a layabout whose only interest lay in squandering the wealth of the Kingdom as if it were his own personal fortune. One has only to look back at the history of the Kings of England since 1066 to see numerous examples of inappropriate leadership produced by the patriarchal system of inheritance which came to replace matrilineal succession - a system whereby Kings claimed to rule by 'Divine-right' rather than by being chosen.

Charles I, for instance, was so taken by the notion of the divine right of Kings that he dismissed Parliament and ruled like a tyrant for eleven years, thus provoking a terrible and bloody civil war before he was eventually removed and executed. George III was insane by the age of 51 but for the next nine years until his death he was still officially the King, even though he was totally incapable of ruling.

With the practice of matrilineal succession, however, where the King was chosen, a man who went mad or did not live up to earlier expectations could be easily relieved of his duties. Amongst the Celts it was important that the

King should be an accomplished warrior capable of leading his men into battle, because the Celtic tribes were notorious for fighting amongst themselves (and still are, if Northern Ireland is anything to go by!).

The survival and wealth of a tribe would be dependant upon its ability to look after itself. A weak or defective King, unable to protect his Kingdom, would be in danger of ruling over a literal wasteland. Any neighbouring tribe would be able to over-run the territory stealing cattle, slaughtering the population and giving the farmers no peace in which to raise their all important crops.

A wounded King, an unpopular King or a King past his prime would simply be unable to fulfil his function satisfactorily and would have to be replaced. We can see this process at work in some of the old Irish legends. For instance, when King Nuadu lost his sword bearing arm in battle the female elders decided that a man called Eochaid Bres should replace him as King, presumably because he was no longer an effective warrior.

Another example comes from the classic tale *'The Cattle Raid of Cooley'* where Queen Nes agreed to marry Fergus mac Roich, the King of Ulster, on condition that her own son Conchobar ruled Ulster for one year. During that year be became so popular that the men of Ulster voted for him to continue as King and so Fergus was stripped of his Kingship. An unpopular King obviously makes a poor leader.

This necessity to have a strong, healthy King able to lead troops into battle and protect the Kingdom led some of the Celts to the practice of making challenges for the right to be King. In a warrior society the leader needs to be the most able warrior. If the current King loses his strength, goes deaf or blind, then it is obvious that a new candidate should be selected. If the current King is merely suspected of not being a good enough warrior, and is merely thought to be losing his nerve in battle or whatever, then the need for replacement might not be so obvious and anyone suspecting that his removal is needed or who considers himself to be a better candidate would have to make an open challenge for power.

Of course this system, like any other power structure, was open to abuse by the unscrupulous who merely wanted power for themselves and there are numerous instances of warriors challenging Kings to battle, killing them and then marrying the Queen in order to legitimise their own rule.

As Gold points out even as late as 840 AD, the *'Annals of Ulster'* record that Feidhlimdh mac Crimthain, King of Ulster, wanted to be King of all Ireland. He challenged Niall Caille, (King of Tara) to battle, defeated him and then kidnapped his Queen in order to seal his right to Kingship over Tara as well as Ulster.

In fact there are numerous instances of Queens being abducted simply in order to provoke the ruling King into battle - a common way to force a challenge for the right to rule.

As we have seen then in this chapter, it was not normal practise amongst the Celts for the position of King to be regarded as a permanent lifelong occupation and this custom arose from the fact that the Celts practised a form of the old Mother Goddess religion. Furthermore, we have also seen that this religion, where the divine being is regarded as female rather than male, gave rise to the tradition that inheritances, including titles, passed through the female line and not the male.

Bearing all this in mind we can now begin to appreciate what kind of effect the new rival religion of Christianity had upon British society in the late 5th Century. Christianity, which holds that the divine being is male and not female, reverses all of these customs and traditions. The female has no place in creation apart from playing a supportive role to the male.

In the Jewish creation myth remember, Adam was made first in God's image and Eve was created just to keep him company and to bear his children. Christianity followed closely the Jewish custom of suppression of the female in favour of the male.

It was this factor that gave Christianity the edge over the old religion as far as a great number of men were concerned. It had so many advantages for the more ambitious man for in any society the most prestigious and powerful jobs are those to be found within either religion or politics and in any society where the Goddess was worshipped these twin peaks of power were effectively controlled by women. Within religion, the top positions of Priestess were reserved for women only because they were meant to represent the Goddess. Within politics a man could become King or leader but actual sovereignty was held by his wife, the Queen and the position of King was by no means guaranteed for life. An ambitious, greedy or power hungry King would always be vulnerable and could be replaced legally.

Christianity on the other hand opened up new avenues of power for men. Right from the very beginning it excluded all women from holding any religious office. It was totally dominated by men because only men could represent the male God. Under a Christian regime society had to become patrilineal with titles and possessions being handed down from father to son. A Christian King could be King in his own right and he could hold the position for life. He was no longer dependant upon the Queen that he married, instead the Queen became dependant upon the King for her position. Moreover, the son of a Christian King could now be certain of becoming King himself one day and no longer needed to seek out a Queen who held sovereignty. This new religion of Christianity changed the course of Arthur's life and the face of British history.

Footnote:
Readers who think that the custom of replacing old Kings with younger and more active men is an inhuman and archaic practise may well stop to consider for a moment what happens in today's modern business world. Throughout Western civilisation, in boardrooms and on factory floors alike, older men are constantly threatened by the new rising stars. As soon as a company hits financial difficulties it is the older man who is sacrificed first. It is the older employee who is made redundant or pushed to one side to make room for the new 'King' with his vitality and his energy and his fresh approach to business (and most importantly his ability to actually use the new computer system that the company has just been conned into buying!) If this replacement procedure is considered good for business now, it was probably considered good for 'business' in the past.

Chapter Four

In the first chapter we briefly reviewed Malory's account of the life and legend of Arthur, pointing out that his version of events has become more or less accepted as the standard version that everyone is familiar with. Along with this generally goes the implicit understanding that the stories take place against a typical Christian background and must therefore be interpreted from the standpoint of Christian morality and ethics. Arthur, who fights his battles under the banner of the cross, is heralded as the greatest of our ancient Christian Kings. The downfall of his Kingdom occurs because his court transgresses Christian moral standards and it can only be saved by a pure Knight who alone is worthy enough to receive a vision of the Holy Grail.

As we have subsequently seen, however, there is a far more complex and mysterious undercurrent at work in these tales than this simple straight-forward Christian explanation would have us believe. Only by examining closely the deeper and older religious themes and social traditions involved can we really hope to understand what takes place in the Arthurian legends for although the

legends were written down between the 12th and 15th century, they refer back to a much earlier time.

This was a time when Britain was poised on the brink of chaos caught between a new world order and the old Celtic ways. Christianity was in its infancy and Saxon invaders fought with Celtic tribes whose stable social order had been so chronically undermined by centuries of Roman occupation. Changes were rapidly taking place in the Britain of the historical Arthur but the backdrop to these changes was the enduring tradition of the Celts.

Only by re-examining the legends in the light of what we now know about the old religion and the customs it gave rise to can we really begin to make sense of the stories of Arthur and the Grail and understand the motives of the people involved.

Perhaps we should start this re-examination right at the beginning and take a closer look at the strange events that surrounded Arthur's birth. Now most of the stories about Arthur have been altered considerably by the various authors involved as time went by, but oddly enough this particular story has remained virtually unchanged since Geoffrey of Monmouth's original account. Uther Pendragon, you may remember, was Arthur's father. He fell madly in love with Igraine who was the wife of Gorlois, 'Duke of Tintagel'. He was so madly in love with Igraine, it seems, that he killed Gorlois, assumed his likeness (with Merlin's help of course) and slept with her. Shortly after this they were married.

By today's standards this whole sequence of events must strike us as odd to say the least. Why on earth should Igraine consent to marry a man like this? Uther

Pendragon murdered the man to whom she had been married for some considerable time (for they had a least three children together). He then deceived her into sleeping with him by the use of sorcery, (which must be considered nowadays as some kind of rape by magic), and then as if this were not enough he gave away the child that she had carried for nine months to some mad magician, presumably in payment for the original deception!

How can all this be explained in ordinary terms? Surely no normal woman would accept behaviour like this and as Igraine was a noble woman, with presumably at least some powerful and influential friends, why did she not attempt to get out of the situation in some way? Either Igraine was as besotted with Uther as he apparently was with her, or there must be some other explanation. Presumably, however, if Igraine had been madly in love with Uther he would never have needed to disguise himself in the first place.

The explanation to all this then must lie elsewhere. The only satisfactory way to understand the whole episode is to see it as an enactment of the ancient Celtic custom of replacing the old King and marrying the Queen. If we add to this custom some of the facts we already know about 5th Century politics, a very clear picture of Uther's motivation emerges. If Gorlois was 'Duke of Tintagel' he probably ruled over a sizeable part of Cornwall. Uther's own territory, however, was in the South of England.

Now remember that at this time the Saxons were invading the South in very large numbers and driving the Celts Westwards. It seems highly likely then that Uther had lost or was about to lose his own territory and was on the look out for a suitable replacement in an area not yet subjected to Saxon mayhem. Cornwall was still a Celtic stronghold and thus must have presented a very attractive proposition for him. However, under Celtic law the only way he could possibly gain a Kingdom in Cornwall would be to depose a reigning King and marry the Queen who held sovereign rights to that particular territory.

Gorlois may have been 'Duke' or 'King' but it was Igraine who held the territorial rights. When we consider these factors is it really surprising that Uther 'fell in love' with her and would stop at nothing to be married. When Uther disposed of Gorlois and slept with Igraine he not only acquired a wife he also acquired a new Kingdom which was not as yet under threat from the invaders.

Celtic tradition then can quite comfortably account for Uther's actions in this affair but what is it that motivates Igraine to accept him as her new husband?

Well, Igraine was a Celtic Queen. As a Princess she must have been brought up in the knowledge that any future husband she might have would be subject to the possibility of sudden replacement by a new King. This possibility must have surely been accepted as a regrettable fact of life by all Celtic Queens - the downside, as it were, of the exalted position as sovereign of their own territory. Igraine would have had to come to terms with the likelihood of it happening well in advance of the actual event. So when it did happen, and Uther successfully challenged Gorlois, she was able to accept Uther as her new husband under Celtic law.

As to the baby Arthur being taken away from her and given to foster parents to bring up, well this too is explainable. It was in fact a well established social custom. Even Julius Caesar remarked upon it when he was compiling his reports about Celtic France just prior to his invasion. Gold points out in his book that the old Irish stories talk about fostering children as though it were a completely natural social practise and in fact the Irish continued to raise their children in this way until long after the Norman invasion of their country. As a custom it was not confined to the Celts alone either because amongst the Norman aristocracy it was practised well into the middle-ages. Apparently, they thought it was much easier to bring up someone else's son than their own, while the Celts in France thought it wrong for boys from the aristocracy to approach their fathers in public until they were old enough to bear arms.

We can only speculate as to why this custom might have developed but one possibility that comes to mind is that if a King's son is fostered out and grows up outside the privileged atmosphere of the ruling family, then he is less likely to see himself as a very special person who deserves to automatically take over the territory when his father dies.

If he has any ambitions himself to be King then he will have to prove himself worthy of the position in the same way that any other man of ambition would. Added to this, of course, is the fact that in a social climate where one's father has to face the possibility of being replaced by a younger rival it would arguably make more sense from the child's point of view if he was not allowed to become too emotionally attached to his real father in the first place.

The next point to consider in the story is the role played by Merlin. He was obviously one of Uther's most trusted advisers. He helped him to gain a new Kingdom and arranged for Arthur to be placed with good foster parents. Merlin has been variously described as a wise-man, a sorcerer or wizard, and a prophet. His mother was Princess and a Priestess of the old religion, while his father is unknown. Indeed some of the more Christianised writers have Merlin's father as a demon or incubus. Robert de Boron, for example, maintained that "...the magician's conception was planned by the Devil and the Lords of Hell. They plotted to ruin mankind by bringing into the world a false prophet, half demon and half man". Apparently, according to de Boron, only the fact that Merlin's mother became a Christian before he was born saved mankind because this had the effect of restraining his evil power!

When he was just a boy, Merlin's gift of second sight saved him from becoming a sacrificial victim. A King by the name of Vortigern, was attempting to build a tower in the Welsh mountains near Snowdon. The tower kept crumbling and he was told that it would only stand if he sacrificed a fatherless child and buried him under the foundation stones.

Hearing that Merlin was a fatherless child, Vortigern had him brought to Snowdon. When Merlin stood before the King, however, he told him that the tower was crumbling because there was a hidden lake deep below the foundations where two dragons lived. When the foundations were dug out the lake was revealed and sure enough there were two dragons inside, one red and the other white. Vortigern, realising that the boy was destined to be very special, spared Merlin's life. Merlin lived for many years as a wild man in the forests of Wales and the North of England. Eventually he became chief adviser to Uther Pendragon and his abilities included, amongst other things, the power to foretell the future and the ability to change shape and assume the form of any animal or bird that he wished.

Clearly, Merlin was no Christian. It seems reasonably to suppose that he was one of the last surviving Druids. They had always been famous for their wisdom and magic and they invariably took on the role of advisers to the aristocracy. Merlin may not have been a Christian but he knew about the Grail because according to several sources it was Merlin who persuaded Uther to construct the Round-Table using the Grail table as a model. So, it was Merlin who really inspired the whole ideal of Arthurian Knighthood and the Grail quest itself.

As Cavendish points out, it is not the Christian Church who inspires the search for the Grail, but Merlin the great enchanter who is thought to be half demon. (Cavendish believes the underlying implication to be that the Grail quest is really something stranger and much older than the Church would like to admit).

If Merlin was indeed a Druid* then he undoubtedly still practised the old religion and thus the young Arthur, to who Merlin also became chief adviser, was much more likely to have been counselled in the ways of the old religion than the Christian Church.

*Footnote: The original Druids were much different from modern day `Druids' who now, apparently, worship the sun amongst other things.

In Malory's version of how Arthur became King, Merlin arranged a contest to see who could withdraw a sword that he had magically placed within a stone anvil. According to Malory this contest took place in a churchyard on Christmas day. Now as everyone knows, the Christian Church takes a very dim view of magical acts, unless that is, they were performed by Jesus or one of his accredited Saints when they are then described as miracles instead.

The notion of a shape-shifting sorcerer performing magic in a churchyard on Christmas day is beyond credibility! Not only would the Church be most aggrieved but also, no self respecting Druid would ever dream of such a thing. If Merlin were to arrange a contest like this to choose a King, surely he would have felt much more at home at Stonehenge or some other such site sacred to the old religion, and he would certainly have arranged it for a Celtic Festival day like Beltain or May Day instead of Christmas.

Clearly, this episode represents an attempt by Malory, de Boron and company to add a Christian flavour to the manner in which Arthur became King. Certainly this famous event is not present in the early versions of the legend. Geoffrey of Monmouth for instance has Arthur simply succeeding his father as King when Arthur came of age (Uther having died when Arthur was still young). What is interesting about Malory's version, however, is that he made it apparent that an actual contest was held to choose a new King (even if it was rigged in Arthur's favour by magic), and as we now know contests for Kingship were a common Celtic practise.

Both Geoffrey and Malory make the point most carefully that Arthur was the 'rightful' King of England. This is a most interesting statement and deserves to be examined closely. If the whole of Britain had been at that time a completely Christian country then Arthur could properly be proclaimed as a 'rightful King' since his father was King before him and patriarchal succession, as we have seen, is one of the main social consequences of Christianity. However, as we have shown, after the fall of the Roman Empire Britain was left in a state close to political and social chaos out of which came a resurgence of the Celtic way of life based squarely upon the matrilineal inheritance which had never been forgotten or truly repressed all through the occupation.

Under Celtic law Arthur had no claim to kingship at all, let alone 'rightful' kingship despite the fact that his father had been a King. In Celtic law if Arthur wanted to be King then he would, like any other ambitious man, have to find a Queen to marry him first. Since Britain was not a Christian country we cannot assume that patriarchal inheritance was the rule and so to discover exactly how Arthur did manage to become a King we must re-examine the events that took place directly after the sword in the stone contest.

According to Malory, the other nobles in the land did not take too kindly to the notion of Arthur being claimed as King and they rebelled against him. Now a leading figure in this rebellion was one Lot of Lothian who had a Kingdom in Scotland. Lot's wife was Morganuse, mother of Gawain, Gaheris and Agravain, but also daughter of Igraine and thus Arthur's half-sister. During a lull in the fighting, Lot apparently sent Morganuse to see Arthur as an ambassador, presumably to try to arrange some kind of a peace treaty. Arthur did not know that she was his half-sister and he slept with her. She conceived a boy who was born on May day and was named Mordred.

Merlin had previously predicted to Arthur that a boy born on May Day would be his downfall, so Arthur desperately tried to arrange for all boys born on May Day to be killed but he was not successful in killing Mordred. When Lot heard about all this, he was so enraged that he resumed hostilities and in the end, after much fighting he was killed in battle by Pellinore, one of Arthur's Knights. Sometime after these events, Arthur had a disagreement with Pellinore which led to a duel and during the ensuing contest, Arthur broke the sword that he had taken from the stone.

Now according to the standard Christianised interpretation of all this, Arthur committed a grievous error by sleeping with Morganuse, even though he did not apparently know who she was. His incestuous son, Mordred, is the one who eventually mortally wounds Arthur in his final battle and the view is taken that this is really Arthur's just reward for having sinned. This interpretation, however, does not help us to understand what is happening here. In particular it does not provide the answers to three very important questions.

Firstly, and most obviously, how did Arthur not know that Morganuse was his half-sister? Admittedly he was fostered out to another family, but he had learned of his real parents before this event took place and in any case Merlin, his adviser, most certainly knew about Morganuse. From the French story of the "Enface Gauvain" we know that Lot was originally Morganuse's page or servant and from Geoffrey of Monmouth we know that he later rose to Uther's commander-in-chief before becoming a Scottish King. Since Merlin was Uther's adviser at this time he must have known both Morganuse and her husband. Surely then he would have informed Arthur that this lady was in fact his half-sister?

The second question that arises is this; if Morganuse was sent as an ambassador, why did she stay with Arthur for so long? Surely a peace treaty would not take nine months to negotiate. Was she reluctant to go back to Lot because of her condition or did she perhaps intend to leave Lot and stay with Arthur for good, until she discovered that Arthur planned to dispose of all babies born on May Day?

Maybe the reason was something more complicated than this. Was Morganuse really more of a hostage than an ambassador? Perhaps she had been seized during the fighting and had to wait until her husband could rescue her or until she could escape. Whatever the reason that made her stay so long, Arthur must have had very good reasons of his own to be so interested in her - considering that they were so closely related and the fact that he was still a young man while she was the mother of three grown sons.

The third main question that arises from the story is this. If Pellinore was one of Arthur's vassals, what prompted the duel that led to Arthur's original sword being broken? Knights generally do not fight with their rightful King unless some really major disagreement is taking place. None of the stories give an account of what happened. Indeed, none of the questions raised here are answered in the stories themselves and neither can they be answered form the point of view of Christian tradition. It seems that something is taking place within these stories which has been purposely glossed over or avoided and this 'something' obviously has to do with the manner in which Arthur became King. Let us therefore re-examine these events, but this time looking at them from the point of view of Celtic tradition.

Arthur as a young man no doubt despised the Saxon invaders and like most other young warriors of the time must have longed to rid the country of them. This hatred would undoubtedly have fuelled his desire to become a King or Chieftain - the only position available at the time to confer enough respect, authority and money to enable anyone to recruit the forces necessary to fight off the invaders. Only a King could raise an army. Presumably also Arthur must have heard stories of the Great Roman Empire and how it brought untold riches and power to its rulers. Maybe Arthur even had ambitions to build such an Empire for himself one day. Whatever his ultimate aim, however, the starting point was the same. He first had to gain control over one of the many small territories that Britain was divided into in those days. Since the Celts had resumed their traditional ways, Arthur would not have had much choice in the way in which this could be done. He had to select a territory, successfully challenge its King for the right to rule and then marry its Queen - just like his father Uther before him had done when he was forced by the Saxons to leave his own Kingdom and take over a new one in Cornwall.

Arthur then must have been on the look out for a suitable Kingdom to make a bid for. One of the most important deciding factors in choosing which Kingdom to take would undoubtedly be the ease with which the present incumbent could be replaced. Another deciding factor at the time would presumably have been its distance from the Saxons (the further away the better!). Lot's Kingdom in Lothian must have been a very tempting proposition. It was situated in Scotland, safely away from the main invasion area and Lot by this time must have been an old man if he had been Uther's commander-in-chief before Arthur was even born.

Lot's wife and Arthur's half-sister was, as we know, called Morganuse but from Geoffrey of Monmouth's account and also from the French *"Enfaces Gavain"* comes the information that her original name was Anna. It seems that the name Morganuse was used to denote the tribal name of the Queen who held sovereignty over that particular part of Scotland (the Orkneys) rather than her personal name. This seems to have been a fairly common occurrence amongst Celtic communities.

For instance, in the Irish stories the name of Queen Medb crops up again and again in different time periods and with many different husbands. The only way to account for the discrepancy is to see the name Medb as a common name given to whichever woman held sovereignty at any one particular time. Another name which seems to have been held in common like this it the more famous one of Gwenivere - a point which we will return to later.

Now if Arthur badly wanted a Kingdom and Lot's Kingdom was thought to be not only safe but also easy to take over, then it must have been too good a proposition to ignore despite the fact that he would have to marry its Queen, and she was his half-sister. A man of ambition would not let a trivial fact like that stand in his way!

We can only conjecture about what might have happened, but if the many stories of abduction are anything to go by we can fairly confidently suppose that the following scenario took place. Arthur, with a loyal warband of warriors must have trekked up to Scotland, somehow snatched Queen Morganuse away and retreated hastily back to some safer territory. The logic behind this abduction routine is presumably to force a King who is reluctant to accept a straight-forward challenge to come out and fight. A King whose wife holds the right of sovereignty obviously cannot remain King for very long without her, so he has to try to get her back if he wants to keep his position.

Arthur slept with Morganuse as a prelude to marrying her (just as Uther did with Igraine) and Morganuse was held until Lot could find out where she was and rally his forces together to attempt a rescue. At this stage, Arthur was half-way to becoming King. He had the Queen and had slept with her so all he had to do now was dispose of Lot. Unfortunately, however, he was never able to complete his take-over bid because he did not kill Lot. Pellinore killed him instead. It seems that Arthur was not the only one interested in Lot's Kingdom!

In Malory's version of events Pellinore is described as one of Arthur's vassals. Other sources, however, have described him as the King of Northumberland or King of the Gaste Forest.

Looking at an ancient map of Britain of the time, it soon becomes apparent that the area around Northumberland was actually taken over by the Saxons and turned into the Saxon Kingdom of Bernicia. Could it be possible that King Pellinore had been relieved of his own Kingdom by the Saxons and was therefore on the look out for another, safer, place to rule? Suppose Pellinore also had his eye on Lot's Kingdom. If so, then Arthur would be a rival. Since Pellinore managed to kill Lot then the only other man to stand in his way of becoming the new King of Lothian was Arthur. Arthur on the other hand had slept with the Queen and so they were now both equal contenders for the Kingship. The only way to decide who would be the next ruler of Lothian would be to fight it out - a duel. As we know, it was precisely in such a duel with Pellinore that Arthur broke the sword that he took from the stone. Presumably, he lost the contest. He never became King of Lothian and was probably lucky to escape with his life.

Pellinore as the victor would have been free now to marry Morganuse and claim Kingship of Lothian. Whether he actually did so is unclear. There is an interesting footnote to this episode however. From the French story "Liore d'Artus" comes the information that Pellinore was also know as the rich Fisher King and that he was 'wounded in the thighs'. Since we have seen before that this is a medieval euphemism for wounded in the genitals perhaps Pellinore was no longer in a fit state to be considered for Kingship by the time all the fighting was over. After all, a new King was expected to be fertile as well as being a warrior. At any rate, according to Malory, Morganuse was still looking for another husband and was actually in the process of trying out Pellinore's son for the position when one of her own sons, Gaheris, discovered them in bed together and killed her! We can only speculate as to what was happening here. Did the injured Pellinore encourage his own son to mate with the Queen determined that someone in the family should be King after all his trouble? Morganuse apparently had no daughters so perhaps Gaheris was rather hoping that he would be able to take over his mother's territory and claim Kingship for himself in view of the changing social climate where the new religion of Christianity was giving its official blessing to patrilineal succession rather than matrilineal. No wonder the stories of Arthur and his court were so popular. They must have been the medieval equivalent of modern day soap operas!

Coming back to Arthur, he must have been bitterly disappointed to have lost his contest with Pellinore. After some two years of plotting and fighting he still had no Queen and therefore no Kingdom under Celtic law and according to Malory he had broken his best sword into the bargain. Of course, at this stage if Arthur was already the rightful King of England, as we have been led to believe, none of this would have mattered very much. He would be a King regardless of the fact that he had no Queen. As Malory makes it clear, however, Arthur was still very anxious to be married. So anxious in fact that he was willing to marry Gwenivere even though Merlin advised him against it. This gives us a further indication of the fact that as a Celt he simply was not acceptable as a King until he married a rightful Queen.

What would Arthur's next step be? He must surely have talked things over with Merlin asking the sage to advise him as to how he could possibly gain a Kingdom now after his defeat at the hands of Pellinore. What advice would Merlin have to offer this would-be King of England?

Chapter Five

According to Malory, what Merlin did next was to find Arthur a new sword! Shortly after the duel with Pellinore Merlin took Arthur to a lake beneath which lived a mysterious fairy woman variously known as Vivianne, Nimue or more simply, the Lady of the Lake.

The Lady of the Lake was a beautiful, magical woman who later on in the stories, came to Arthur's rescue several times. To describe her as a fairy really creates the wrong impression because we are now accustomed to thinking of 'fairies' as insipid, frivolous or dainty little creatures. The original meaning of the word 'fairy' however, is completely different. A fairy or fay, was, as Cavendish points out, a powerful immortal being whose true home is in the 'otherworld'. Sometimes these beings (usually women) are born into human families if they choose but they retain their magic powers and can be ruthless, unpredictable and often cruel in their dealings with ordinary humans. Clearly, a fairy or fay is not to be taken lightly although this particular Lady was well disposed towards Arthur.

The question we have to consider of course is this. Is the Lady of the lake simply a benevolent fay who decided to help Arthur because she liked the look of him or is there a deeper significance to all this that needs to be uncovered? Also, another question springs to mind. Why should Arthur receive a new sword from the hand of a female lake person? Would it not have been more usual to receive a new sword from some master smith or swordsmaker? After all there are plenty of legends around telling of the magical abilities of smiths such as the famous Wayland for instance. The fact that Arthur's new magic sword comes directly from the hands of a woman, and moreover a woman so closely connected with water, must have some special significance here.

Magical swords do occur fairly frequently in Celtic folklore, which is only to be expected of course since the Celts were so very fond of fighting and a magic sword would obviously be a very useful weapon to have. Bran the Blessed, for instance, took a magical sword him when he went to Ireland. Even broken swords seem to be significant as they figure in the Grail stories as we have seen. The idea of a sword coming out of water, however, would seem to be more puzzling if it were not for the fact that recently archaeologists have actually been finding swords and other weapons of Celtic origin at the bottom of old rivers and on the beds of ancient lakes.

Ross and Robins comment that many such finds have been made in the last few years including one large cache of weapons uncovered from the site of a lake on the Isle of Anglesey. This find dates from around the time of the Druids last stand against the invading Romans. They suggest that throwing weapons, especially swords, into stretches of water may have had a special religious significance for the Celts. Perhaps this was a form of votive offering after winning or (in the case of Anglesey) losing a battle. Whatever the reason, the practise seems to have been a well established custom since such discoveries have been made in many places around Britain and in mainland Europe.

If we now add to these facts some of the information we already know about the Celtic Mother Goddess the picture starts to become a little clearer. In several of Her forms, the Mother Goddess was closely associated with water. Sulis/Minerva for example, was as we saw earlier, worshipped at springs, wells and lakes. These sites were considered sacred places and if swords and other weapons were cast into them as votive offerings on special occasions then the offerings must have been made to the Goddess as Minerva.

Now if the Goddess was offered swords on special occasions is it not possible that on other special occasions she might well decide to offer a sword back in return? A special magical sword for a future King perhaps? It is not too big a leap of imagination to see that the mysterious Lady of the Lake with the magic powers is really none other than the Goddess Minerva or Sulis herself. When Merlin took Arthur to the lake then, he was actually taking him to meet with the Goddess. Obviously Merlin realised that Arthur was in need of some Divine intervention.

What advice did Merlin give to Arthur before he took him to the lake? Let us suppose for a moment that Merlin had been a Christian cleric or monk and Arthur had asked him how on earth he could become a King after his initial attempt had failed so abysmally. We would probably expect Merlin to say something like this "Put it in the hands of God my son, He alone can make you King". However, Merlin, as we know, was no Christian. He was a Druid and the son of a Celtic Priestess with a thorough knowledge of Celtic tradition and law. It is not unreasonable for us to suppose that he was himself a staunch believer in the power of the Goddess so for him it would be the Goddess who decided who became King and who did not. After all, Celtic Kingship was based squarely upon the model of the Goddess and the young-God.

In the Celtic religion the Goddess was the maker and breaker of Kings, not the Christian male-God. Merlin's advice to the young Arthur would then undoubtedly have been something like "Put it in the hands of the Goddess, my friend. It is She alone who decides in these matters".

Merlin, then, would have encouraged Arthur to seek the aid of the Goddess if he really wanted to become King. So he took Arthur to one of the Goddess's Sacred sites and here, presumably, Arthur must have pledged himself to her.

We can imagine the young Arthur vowing to be a loyal subject, ever willing to do the Goddess's bidding if only She would in return help him to fulfil his ambition to be a King. The Goddess must surely have responded to this, for when Minerva gave Arthur a magic sword which could not be broken, was She not actually conferring Kingship upon him? After all, if a man has to fight to become a King in the first place, then a magic sword which cannot be beaten or broken in combat is surely a passport to success. It more or less guarantees that in any future combat or duel he will always be the victor. If Arthur challenged anyone or anyone challenged him for the right to be King he could be certain of winning. As a further guarantee, the scabbard itself would protect him from bleeding to death should he incur any wounds. If by the gift of Excalibur the Goddess had given Arthur Her blessing how could he fail to become King now? Sure enough we read in Malory that shortly after Arthur received Excalibur he 'fell in love' with the beautiful Gwenivere and wanted to marry her.

Geoffrey of Monmouth says Gwenivere was the daughter of a Roman-British aristocratic family but most other sources inform us that she was a British Princess. Malory writes of her as the daughter of a King - Leodegrance of Cameliard; in 'Diu Crone' she is the daughter of King Garlin of Galore. It is the Welsh tradition, though, that is perhaps the most interesting here. The Welsh form of the name Gwenivere is Gwenhwgfar and according to some of the ancient Welsh poems Gwenhwyfar had three fathers. In fact, the source has Arthur marrying three Queens all named Gwenhwyfar and each one had a different father. This is very reminiscent of the way that the name of Queen Medb keeps occurring in the Irish stories and as we mentioned earlier, the best way to account for the repetition is to view the name as a kind of official title for the woman who holds the sovereignty over a particular area.

In the case of the name Gwenhwyfar that area would presumably be a large part of Britain including parts of Wales and Cornwall. It is interesting to note that in the Irish stories, Queen Medb has a daughter called Finnabair and, according to Gold, Finnabair is the Irish equivalent to the Welsh Gwenhwyfar. He suggests that Gwenivere is a title meaning something like eldest daughter of the Queen or dauphin, or she who bestows the Kingdom.

It seems highly probable then that Gwenivere was in Celtic law the woman holding the sovereignty of Britain and that Arthur at last became King by virtue of the fact that he managed to marry her. Cavendish suggests that Arthur's wife came to be regarded as a personification of the land of Britain, the land which Arthur 'married' in his capacity as King.

We would, however, argue that as far as the Celts were concerned, Gwenivere had always been regarded in this way. Consider for instance a story by Caradoc of Llancarfan which appears in the *'Black Book of Carmarthen'* dated around 1099. It tells of how the evil Prince Melwas of Somerset abducted Gwenivere and held her prisoner at Glastonbury. Arthur had to search for a whole year to find her and finally managed to rescue her by laying siege to the Prince's castle. It should be fairly obvious to the reader by now that Celtic Queens were not abducted for their beauty alone - a far more important factor being the territorial rights they could bestow upon a new husband.

It seems fairly clear then that Gwenivere should rightly be regarded as the true sovereign of Britain and that Arthur only became King of Britain when he married her and not before. Most importantly for our understanding of the legends, this marriage did not take place until after Arthur had pledged himself to the Goddess at the lakeside. In other words, the Goddess allowed and indeed helped Arthur to become King, presumably on the understanding that he would continue to be a faithful servant and uphold the practice of Her religion.

It is at this point in Malory's version of the legend that Arthur's chief adviser is suddenly taken away from him.

The great sorcerer Merlin fell madly in love with an enchantress known as Vivienne. She captivated him so much that he gladly taught her all he knew about magic, but she used this against him and managed to imprison him in an ice cavern somewhere in the 'otherworld' where he remains in a state of suspended animation.

Vivienne or Nimue, as she is sometimes known, is thought to have been the Lady of the Lake herself. In the 'Suite du Merlin' Merlin falls in love with the Lady of the Lake who is portrayed as a beautiful huntress dressed in Green. She bursts into Arthur's court one day complete with bow and arrow and Merlin is entranced. This, of course, is a further indication that the Lady of the Lake should be regarded as a Goddess for the description of her closely resembles one of the famous Roman forms of the Goddess as Diana, the huntress. In this story she eventually binds Merlin with a magic girdle and imprisons him in a tomb deep in the woods.

Why would the Lady of the Lake want to take Merlin away from Arthur's side? He was after all presumably one of the Goddess's best supporters, given the fact that he was a Druid. Furthermore, as Christianity was setting itself up as a rival religion surely the Goddess would have wanted as many followers of the Old Religion around as possible?

There is another odd factor to take into consideration here as well. After Arthur received Excalibur he seems to have married Gwenivere rather quickly. There is no mention of him having to fight anyone for the right to be Gwenivere's husband. In fact, she does not seem to have been married to anyone else at the time so there was no need for him to challenge anyone. As he had struggled for almost two years to try to take over Lot's territory, this sudden marriage to Gwenivere seems very easy indeed. Perhaps Merlin suspected that something strange was going on because he actually warned Arthur not to marry the lady. Remember that Merlin could foretell the future, so maybe he realised that there was trouble in store for Arthur.

The Goddess, of course, would be fully aware of Merlin's powers. It seems likely, therefore, that She wanted him out of the way so that Arthur would have to stand on his own two feet and make his own decisions without the aid of someone who knew what was about to happen. Could the Goddess be about to test Arthur's loyalty towards Her? If so, then the presence of Merlin would surely be a hindrance to Her plans because he would always be able to advise Arthur of the best course of action to take. It would make sense, therefore, to remove Merlin from the scene before any such testing began. Thus She set a trap for Merlin and even the best sorcerer in the land, who must have known what was about to happen, could not resist the charms of the Goddess.

With Merlin gone, another player entered into the stories - a young Knight called Lancelot. Lancelot is also known as Lancelot of the Lake. This is because when he was a small child, his mother left him at a lakeside after the death of his father and he was taken away and raised by the Lady of the Lake herself. He never knew who his real parents were. According to some stories, Lancelot was the son of a King called Ban. Under patrilineal succession, of course, this would automatically make Lancelot a King himself, or at least a Prince if he was not the eldest son.

Lancelot, however, was brought up in the Celtic tradition and there is no mention of him having a title. His name has been linked with the Irish God, Lugh, who was a mighty warrior sent from the underworld to help human beings. Lugh too was fostered and trained by a Goddess. As Cavendish remarks, other hero's of Irish and Welsh legends, including Cuchulain and Peredur, were trained in wisdom and war by women, and this seems to be an echo of a real Celtic custom.

Cavendish goes on to add that a hero brought up without a father is his own man, not subjected to the influence of other men in his formative and impressionable years. The fact that he was also brought up amongst women implies that he was initiated into the deeper mysteries of life - an initiation that most men do not receive.

Lancelot then, was brought up in the Old Celtic ways and since he was raised by the Goddess, he could only be equated with the son of the Goddess or the young-God. When he came of age, the Lady of the Lake took him to Arthur's court where he became his best Knight.

So far we have seen all of the main characters who appear in the Arthurian legends with the notable exception of one. Perhaps the most intriguing of them all is Arthur's other half-sister, the notorious Morgan-Le-Fay. It is well known that Morgan-Le-Fay disliked Arthur intensely and went to great lengths to try to bring about his destruction or failing that, at least to try to drive a wedge between Arthur and his Queen.

In the stories themselves there is no satisfactory explanation to account for Morgan's apparent hatred of Arthur. Some modern authors have put forward their own explanations as to why she should behave like this towards her brother, such as the fact that she may have blamed him for her father's death, or that she may have been intensely jealous of his popularity. Both of these may have elements of truth about them, but they are not nearly deep enough or far reaching enough to really account for Morgan's actions.

As her name suggest, Morgan is another of the Fays - those mysterious magical beings who belong to the 'otherworld' but are born from time to time amongst mortals. According to some sources she learnt her magic from Merlin, but presumably if she was a Fay she would have had her own magic anyway. She was an enchantress and a shape-shifter, mostly appearing as a very beautiful woman, but she was capable of changing herself into an old hag, or a stone or whatever suited her purposes best at the time. She could also fly and had powers of healing.

We first met Morgan in Geoffrey of Monmouth's 'Vita Merlin' where she was the ruler of the 'Fortunate Isle' (thought to be Avalon), and it was here that Arthur was taken after his last battle.

Morgan was the leader of a group of nine women and used her healing powers to look after Arthur. This is, of course, a complete contrast to the way in which she was portrayed later on in the stories when her chief intention seemed to have been to make sure that Arthur was killed one way or another. This is another of those discrepancies which needs careful consideration if we are to understand exactly what was happening.

As usual, it does not help very much to try to explain things from an ordinary Christian point of view. Since the legend of Adam and Eve appeared in the Bible, men have been accustomed to seeing even 'nice' women as one step away from evil anyway so a woman such as Morgan is beyond the pale right from the start. If Morgan-Le-Fay was simply the personification of evil out to do away with successful men why should she have been interested in looking after Arthur when he had been mortally wounded? Maybe Christian opinion would say that she had a change of heart and felt sorry for what she had done to him, trying to make up for it by looking after him. A guilty conscience or a conversion to the faith perhaps? Given Morgan's track record, this does not seem very likely. From the point of view of Celtic tradition and the Goddess Religion there are many more plausible explanations for what took place. (The actual events themselves we will consider in the following chapter).

This particular type of woman has a long accredited history amongst the Celtic peoples (as indeed she does amongst other peoples!); the idea of a group of women living alone on an island, for instance, is far from fanciful. A first Century Roman geographer called Pomponius Mels referred to a group of nine such women living on an island off the coast of Brittany. It was claimed that they could heal the sick, foretell the future and even control the weather. These women were Priestesses, women of the Goddess religion.

Nine was a much favoured number of the Celts. In the Welsh poem 'The Spoils of Annwyn' there are nine maidens who look after a magic cauldron, and all around the British countryside there are numerous standing stone circles which are even today still known by the name of 'The Nine Maidens'.

The importance of the number nine is that it is the result of the multiplication of three times three, and three was considered the most sacred number of all by the Celts. The number three refers directly to the Goddess. Long before the Christians discovered 'The Father, The Son and The Holy Ghost', the Goddess worshipping peoples of the world recognised the triple nature of the Goddess. She was revered in three aspects as the Mother, the Maid and the Crone. Now on the surface this obviously refers to the three different stages of life that all women pass through - the youthful maiden, the nurturing loving mother and the older, wise woman who has passed childbearing age. In terms of theology, however, the threefold aspect of the Goddess is a little more complex.

The nurturing loving Mother is of course the Goddess in Her role as Creatress - the Mother who gives life to us all and cares for us and for the rest of Her creation. The youthful Maiden is the aspect of the Goddess who enjoys the life that She has created and takes part in its continuing process. The Crone, on the other hand, takes more understanding.

If the Mother is the Creatress, then the Crone must be seen as the destroyer. This is the one aspect of the Goddess that causes so much anxiety, particularly amongst men. Without this aspect, though, life as we know it could not exist.

The whole of life is a constant flowing process of change. Things come into being, they grow, develop, mature and then finally disintegrate back into formlessness. This timeless law of change applies to everything around us - human life, animal life, plant life, even the Earth and the Universe itself. All have a beginning and will finally have an end. If this process of development and change did not occur there would be nothing new in the world. If everything remained unaltered throughout time then life would stagnate. There would be no changing seasons, no spring flowers, no new born lambs, indeed there would be no children of any kind for humans or animals. To make sure that stagnation does not occur, the process of change and development is vital but this means that the old has to be removed to make way for the new.

If the Goddess in her Mothering aspect gives birth to and nurtures her Creation then the Goddess in her Crone aspect looks after the other side of the process. The Crone represents the death and destruction at the end of things. The removal of the old allows room for the new. It is the Crone who makes sure that life always has meaning and value. She sees to it that it never becomes dull and repetitive. The Crone provides danger, excitement, temptation, obstacles to overcome, fears to conquer, sometimes tragedy and pain, but always She makes sure that life flows and changes. Without this darker, hidden side to Creation there would be no balance in life. Darkness has its part to play no matter how much we might fear or resent it, for without it we would never fully appreciate the majesty of creation.

In this context the Crone aspect of the Goddess is often thought of as the Dark Goddess and has been worshipped under many names throughout the ages. Names such as Kali, Hecate, and the Celtic Kerrigan and the Morrigan. At first sight it might seem strange to actually worship the darker side of the Goddess but the fact is that this darker side must be accepted and respected as an integral and indispensable part of the whole creation process because life never consists of light alone.

This is, of course, where the doctrine of Christianity is so misleading. Its continual emphasis upon light, love and eternal happiness is noble and uplifting but it does not provide a true reflection of creation and life. Nature is at once beautiful and frightening. A warm gentle breeze can become a mindless destructive cyclone in minutes, the strong supportive earth can shake and give way without warning, swallowing up whole acres of civilisation in terrifying earthquakes while disease and famine can wipe out generations of lovingly and carefully raised families in months. None of this can be explained adequately with a one sided view of the Creator.

If the Christians claim that their male God is responsible for the Creation of life why are they afraid to acknowledge that He must also be ultimately responsible for its destruction. If He planned life then He must also have planned death. Christian theologians try to deny this of course, by claiming that death was introduced into the life process as a result of the Adam and Eve incident. This was God's punishment because Adam listened to Eve rather than obeying the command of God, but the life process was already well under way by the time this happened though otherwise there would be no apples on the tree of life for Eve to pick. To maintain that death was introduced as a result of Adam's willingness to take notice of Eve is obvious nonsense unless of course the story was meant to be taken as a symbol of the early rivalry between the Goddess religion, as represented by Eve and the serpent, and the new male God religion.

Ever since this myth was first formulated the Jews, Christians and later the Moslems have done their best to subjugate women especially in the area of religious worship. Women in general have been regarded as potentially evil or dangerous creatures, particularly those who happen to be rather attractive. They are often described by words such as enchanting, bewitching, fascinating - all the words with magical connotations. Morgan-Le-Fay of course was just such a woman.

Cavendish makes the point that Morgan-Le-Fay personified the deep rooted male fear of the evil of women which is to be found at the heart of the Judaeo-Christian tradition - a tradition which is shared by most of the Arthurian writers.

Morgan represents the dark side of the Goddess. The unknown author of "*Sir Gawain and the Green Knight*" described her as 'Morgan the Goddess'. The '*Arthurian Encyclopedia*' has her descended from the Celtic Goddesses Modron, Macha and the Morrigan (although some writers dispute the latter). The Morrigan in particular was a fearsome creature known as the Queen of nightmares. She loved to wander around the battlefield in the shape of a huge crow and pick the flesh from the bones of the dead.

Morgan-Le-Fay is the enchanter, the agent provocateur who stirred up the complacency of Arthur's court. Take for instance her role in the tale of 'Sir Gawain and the Green Knight'. One feast day a Green Knight rode into Arthur's court and laid down a challenge to anyone who dared to behead him. The challenge was taken up by Gawain who agreed to try to cut off the Knight's head with one blow and then to travel to the Green Knight's castle one year later to receive a similar blow in return. Gawain cut off the Green Knight's head with one blow but instead of dying the Green Knight picked up his head and rode away. One year later, Gawain set off for the Green

Knight's castle. One the way he was offered hospitality by a Knight who went out hunting every day leaving Gawain alone with his beautiful wife. Egged on by an ugly old hag, the Knight's wife tried for three days to seduce Gawain but without success.

The hunting Knight is really the Green Knight and he had been testing Gawain. When Gawain offered his head for the return blow, the Green Knight merely gave him a small cut and thus spared his life on the grounds that Gawain refused to sleep with his wife. The ugly old hag turned out to be Morgan-Le-Fay in disguise. She had conceived the whole plot in order to discredit Arthur and his Knights (presumably she had hoped that Arthur would play the game instead of Gawain, but as we shall see, Arthur did not like accepting challenges).

If Morgan-Le-Fay was the personification of the dark Goddess then the Lady of the Lake represents the opposite, light side of the Goddess. Morgan was destructive and cruel while the Lady of the Lake was protective, generous and motherly. When we consider that the Goddess generally had three aspects then obviously Gwenivere was the candidate for the role of Maid. Indeed, Welsh tradition seems to have treated her very much like a Goddess.

In one of the Welsh poems she is referred to as the 'White Goddess'. If this is the case then the three women who were most influential in Arthur's adult life were no less than the three different aspects of the Great Celtic Mother Goddess Herself. The Mother gave him Her support in his bid to become King. The Maid actually confers Kingship upon him by marrying him, while the dark side of the Goddess disliked him intensely and was continually plotting his downfall and death. In the end, however, it was this dark side of the Goddess who took him away to Avalon ostensibly to heal him.

So far then we have been able to demonstrate that when we examine things from the point of view of Celtic tradition the discrepancies and the unexplainable events which occur in Arthurian legends begin to fall into place and become much clearer. It is the only way of looking at the legends that can explain why Uther and Igraine acted so strangely.

It is the only way that explains why Arthur seduced his half-sister, why he fought with Pellinore and why he received Excalibur from the Lady of the Lake. None of these things are understandable in terms of the more accepted interpretation of the Legends. The Christianised point of view is entirely inadequate in this respect. There are, however, still some important questions that remain unanswered.

Firstly, if as we maintain, the legend is much more understandable in terms of Celtic tradition, how is it that Arthur has achieved such a long lasting reputation as a Christian King? Surely we would expect him to be remembered as a Great Celtic warrior King instead? Secondly, if Arthur was indeed honoured by the Goddess and She helped him to become a King why did Morgan, who represented Her darker side, hate him so much that she continually tried to destroy him? It is the answers to these two questions that we will be looking for in the next chapter.

Chapter Six

One day sometime after Arthur became King, Morgan-Le-Fay persuaded him to let her have Excalibur and its magic scabbard for a while. Using her own magic Morgan made an exact copy of the weapon and gave it to Arthur, keeping the original for herself. Shortly after Arthur went out hunting deep in the forest. Becoming separated from his companions he stopped at a river to drink and a ship sailed into the bank at his feet. Being curious he climbed aboard and was greeted by twelve maidens who served him a delicious meal. Presently he fell asleep and awoke to find himself a prisoner in a dark dungeon along with many other Knights. The dungeon was in a castle which belonged to the evil Lord Damas. Morgan-Le-Fay had sent the magic ship to ensnare him.

Damas was in dispute with his brother over some land and was looking for a champion to fight against his brother's champion. He promised to free Arthur if he would accept the challenge on his behalf. Arthur was not very happy about this but agreed in order to regain his freedom. Unfortunately, however, the opposing champion was Morgans lover, the Knight Accolon and she had given him the real Excalibur and scabbard. Arthur's fake sword was no match for Excalibur and soon he was wounded and losing a lot of blood. His sword broke and Accolon demanded that he yield, but Arthur declared that he would rather die with honour than live on in shame. It was then that the Lady of the Lake appeared and came to his rescue. Using her magic she made Excalibur fly through the air into the hands of its rightful owner, and the tables turned on Accolon. Accolon surrendered and told Arthur all about Morgan's scheme. Arthur spared his life, but he died of his wounds some days later.

Sometime after this incident Morgan tried to steal Excalibur again. She waited until Arthur was asleep and tried to pull the sword away from him but he held it tightly even in his sleep and she only managed to take the scabbard. She rode off quickly with her Knights but Arthur awoke and pursued her. He had almost caught up with her when Morgan suddenly threw the scabbard into a nearby lake and quickly turned herself and her Knights into large stones. Thinking that she had been turned to stone as a punishment Arthur rode away. As soon as he had gone Morgan and the Knights came to life once more and rode off to the safety of her castle. Arthur still had Excalibur, but was now without its magical scabbard.

It was Morgan's manipulations that resulted in the duel with Accolon, a duel that almost cost Arthur his life if it had not been for the timely intervention of the Goddess. Arthur had had a bad experience of duelling before when he lost the contest with Pellinore. This second duel probably unnerved him considerably. Now through Morgan's actions again he had permanently lost part of his magical protection. A very important part at that because the magical scabbard would have prevented him from bleeding to death. So in any future contest he would now be vulnerable and would have to trust in the power of the Goddess to protect him directly rather than relying upon the more personal protection of his scabbard.

Morgan-Le-Fay threw the scabbard into a lake. Now remember that Excalibur and its scabbard came out of a lake in the first place so in a very real sense it was returned back to the Lady of the Lake or the Goddess. If we also remember that Morgan-Le-Fay represents the darker side of the Goddess then it seems more than likely that the Goddess decided to make Arthur more vulnerable on purpose and that Morgan was the instrument used to accomplish this. Was the Goddess testing Arthur's loyalty towards Her and his trust in Her ability to look after him? If so, then Morgan-Le-Fay's actions can be seen in a new light.

Morgan did not act simply out of jealousy or hatred towards Arthur but she was acting on behalf of the Goddess, creating situations and tensions through which Arthur's actions and motives could be tested. This role as the 'doer of dark deeds' on behalf of the Goddess was not confined to creating awkward situations for Arthur though, as we shall see later on when we look at what happened to Lancelot and Gwenivere. As far as Arthur was concerned, his first test was the affair with the fake Excalibur and Accolon. Presumably the Goddess must have been fairly pleased with the way in which he acquitted himself because She stepped in at the very last moment to save him after he had decided he would rather die with honour than live with shame.

It seems, however, that this one test was not sufficient to demonstrate his loyalty and faith for although he had a fake Excalibur, Arthur believed that he had the real thing and could thus afford to fight heroically without fear of dying. How would he react now knowing that his magical Scabbard was gone? Would he still be a valiant and fearless warrior ready to do the Goddess's bidding or would he opt out and decide it was all too much for him? The Goddess wanted to test him again but before She did so another incident occurred just to reassure him as it were that She could be trusted to look after him no matter what was happening.

One day at the court an enchantress managed to slip a magical ring onto Arthur's finger. It robbed him of his memory and she took him away from Camelot. However, the Lady of the Lake quickly sent some of her female servants to rescue him. They followed the enchantress, removed the ring and Arthur regained his memory completely.

Maybe by this time, though, Arthur was beginning to have second thoughts about the Goddess and Her ways. Maybe he always did have reservations which is probably why She decided to test him in the first place. Arthur's most telling test, however, was just about to begin. In true Celtic fashion someone made a challenge to Arthur's right to be King. The earliest account of the events come from Chrètien de Trôyes in his 'Lancelot'.

One Ascension Day (Spring time or Beltaine in the Celtic calendar) Meleagant, Prince of Gorre, carried off Queen Gwenivere and took her to his father's castle. To get his Queen back and keep his Kingdom under Celtic traditions Arthur obviously had to fight for her. Arthur, however, did nothing. Meleagant even came back to Camelot and boasted about all the other prisoners he had taken from

Arthur's Kingdom but Arthur merely said he had no power to do anything about it. Was he afraid to fight now that he had lost the scabbard? It must have been a shock to him after all when it was stolen from him and not returned. Lancelot and Gawain had no reservations, however, and they both set off in pursuit of Meleagant in order to rescue Gwenivere.

Chrètien de Trôyes' story of the abduction of Gwenivere is very similar to the abduction story in the *Life of Gildas* by Caradoc of Llancarfen which was mentioned earlier. In Caradoc's tale, however, it was Arthur who rescued Gwenivere from the clutches of Melwas. Because the name Melwas is similar to Meleagant it has generally been assumed that Chrètien's story is a variation of this earlier tale of Caradoc's with Lancelot as the hero instead of Arthur. This is, of course, a distinct possibility, but there also remains the other possibility that there might have been two separate incidents. The first time Arthur rescued Gwenivere, but the second time he decided not to.

In the 'first' abduction Gwenivere's rescue was accomplished by means of a siege. Arthur's men surrounded the castle and presumably starved Melwas into surrendering. In Chrètien de Trôyes story, however, Meleagant made a more personal challenge to the King which needed, for honour's sake, to be answered by personal combat. This was much more in keeping with the old Celtic ways, of course, and perhaps something that Arthur was growing tired of.

When Meleagant appeared at Arthur's court bragging about Gwenivere and the other prisoners that he had taken, Arthur merely said that he had no power to make him return them. Yet he still had Excalibur, his magical sword which could not be beaten in combat. Surely he could have been fairly confident of accepting the challenge and winning the duel? He should also have been confident that the Goddess would help him out if he needed it because She had helped him out before. After all, the Celtic ways were based upon the Goddess religion and it was the Goddess who had made him King in the first place.

By not accepting the challenge he was breaking faith not only with his Celtic tradition but also with the Goddess Herself. By his inaction he made it clear that he no longer considered it necessary to fight for his Queen and the sovereignty that she represented. In other words, at this point he must have started to consider himself a King in his own right and was no longer too concerned about what happened to Gwenivere.

In the absence of Merlin was Arthur now taking council from some Christian advisor? Was he being assured that the true Creator was not the Goddess but the Christian God and that matrilineal succession was no longer important? Was he now being assured that he could be considered a King in his own right due to the fact that his father before him was also a King? Maybe Arthur was now taking the first steps along the road to Christianity.

Lancelot and Gawain, meanwhile, were very concerned about Gwenivere. On discovering there were two separate ways to enter the Kingdom of Gorre they split up and travelled alone. Before long Lancelot's horse died and after some hesitation he decided to accept a lift in a cart normally used to transport condemned men to the gallows. This was a very humiliating experience for the Knight and caused much laughter amongst the ordinary people.

When he finally reached the land of Gorre he discovered that the only bridge across the river to get to the castle was made of swords set on edge. He was forced to crawl across on his hands and knees and was cut badly. Despite his wounds he immediately challenged Meleagant and was just about to defeat him when Meleagant's father pleaded with Gwenivere to stop the fight. Meleagant agreed to set Gwenivere free on condition that the contest could be resumed at a later date. Lancelot agreed to this and Gwenivere was freed. She was not very pleasant towards Lancelot for some time though. Apparently she had heard about how he hesitated before accepting a ride in the Executioner's cart and this displeased her. By the time they returned to the court, however, they were on much friendlier terms but it was not until sometime later that they actually became lovers according to Chrètien de Trôyes' account.

Now in the normal course of events under the Celtic tradition if Lancelot had slept with the Queen after rescuing her then he would be a principle contender for the position of King. He would only need to challenge Arthur and win to become the Queen's new husband. This did not happen so Arthur had in essence been given another chance. Lancelot was obviously not contending for the Kingship, and Meleagant was still alive and threatening to lay down challenges in the future. Presumably then the whole test could happen all over again if necessary. Perhaps the Goddess was hoping that Arthur would come to his senses and go after Gwenivere the next time if the test was resumed. She obviously did not want him to embrace Christianity without giving him another chance to prove himself as a man of the Goddess. Was Arthur hovering on the brink of indecision then at this point in his life?

Was he contemplating whether he should be giving up the Goddess religion for ever and take on Christianity completely? If so, this would have a tremendous impact not only on his life but also on the lives of everyone around him. The Celts had followed the Goddess's ways since time immemorial and She would not be willing for him to take such a decisive step without leaving him at least an opening to come back to Her if he wanted to try again.

Unfortunately, however, it seems that Arthur did not avail himself of this second chance. He began fighting off the Saxons and as a very early historical source informs us, Arthur went into battle under the banner of the cross. This must have displeased the Goddess intensely because before very long Arthur was a prisoner once more and Lancelot and Gwenivere became lovers. While Arthur was fighting the Saxons he was seduced by the enchantress Camille, the sister of a Saxon King. She lured him into a castle and held him captive in a dungeon. That same night Lancelot slept with Gwenivere for the first time. Camille sent word to Arthur's court that he was being held and Lancelot, Gawain and other Knights set out to rescue him. Unfortunately, by means of some clever trickery, they too were captured and held in the same dungeon as Arthur.

Separated from Gwenivere, Lancelot went mad and Camille let him go thinking that he was no longer a threat to anyone. The Lady of the Lake, however, came to his rescue. She restored his sanity and gave him a magical ring which could break all spells and with this he was able to return to Camille's castle to release Arthur and the other Knights.

These events without doubt marked a turning point in Arthur's life. As a Celtic King it was really the beginning of his downfall. Up until this point in his life he had had no really serious threat to his position as King. Now Lancelot, the best Knight in the land was the Queen's lover and thus just one step away from challenging him for the right to be Gwenivere's next husband. Moreover, this same Lancelot had been raised by the Lady of the Lake Herself and so must have been quite special to Her. Ever since Arthur had first become King the Lady of the Lake had intervened directly on his behalf when he needed help. Now, however, She intervened not for Arthur but for Lancelot. It was he who received the magical ring and it was left up to him to decide whether or not to rescue Arthur. Clearly then, Arthur should have looked upon these events as a warning for obviously Lancelot was beginning to replace him in the Goddess's affections as well as in Gwenivere's.

It would seem then that just before the encounter with Camille Arthur had finally decided to abandon the Celtic religion and turn instead to Christianity. What was Arthur's motive for this apparent change of heart? Why would a man who owed his very position as King to the existence and benevolence of one religion turn his back upon that religion and embrace a rival one? Was it because he 'saw the light' and suddenly recognised Christianity as the one true meaningful religion and the Christian God as the true creator?

Genuine religious conversions do occur from time to time, of course, but if Arthur's conversion was a truly religious experience we could reasonably expect him to have changed his lifestyle a little to fit in with his new beliefs. We would not necessarily expect him to have become a monk because he could easily claim to be doing 'God's work' by remaining a King and ridding the country of the Saxons. Would we, however, expect a newly converted King with strong Christian convictions and a high sense of honour and moral duty to keep hold of a magical sword given to him by the Goddess? Surely the decent thing to do would at least have been to throw Excalibur back into the lake where it came from. That act alone would have made it clear that from now on his trust would be in his new God and his new religion instead of in the Goddess and Her religion.

Arthur, however, did no such thing. He fought under the banner of the cross with the magical sword given to him by the Goddess. Arthur's conversion to Christianity was not a religious experience at all, it was a matter of expediency. Arthur wanted to be a King in his own right and only Christianity could offer him that. The Goddess had made him a King but the price he had to pay was the acceptance of Her and Her ways. He had to prove himself worthy of the position of King as often as necessary. He had to be open to challenges from rivals and trust in the Goddess to help him win. This meant, of course, he had to demonstrate that he was a loyal and faithful servant to Her or presumably She would not help him. The Goddess had been testing his loyalty with the help of Morgan to see whether he was a worthy servant or whether he was simply interested in being a King.

By switching to Christianity Arthur was attempting to hold on to his position as King for as long as possible. Under Christianity there was no need for him to accept personal challenges from his rivals. He would not have to fight to keep his Queen unless he really wanted to because under patrilineal succession he would be King in his own right no longer dependant upon his Queen and the sovereignty she represented. Was this to him more important than his religion? Was he willing to turn his back upon the Goddess for the chance to make his Kingship a permanent fixture, regardless of Gwenivere?

Not that Christian Kings were immune to challenges for their positions, however. History is littered with territorial wars of one sort or another and Kings were replaced frequently. The difference between these affairs and the Celtic challenge for Kingship lies in the fact that the former are actual wars or battles in which thousands of ordinary people lose their lives. The Celtic tradition was enshrined as a personal duel between two men each trying to prove himself worthy of the position of King. One the younger challenger, the other usually the reigning King fighting to retain or gain the right to the Queen and to gain access to the sovereignty she held. In a patrilineal society any attempt to gain access to the territory of a ruling King results in a mass battle between two opposing armies.

Under patrilineal succession the man who became the King or leader was the one who could raise and command the largest and most ferocious army. It was no longer a personal affair between two warriors, instead it involved a tremendous amount of wasted lives and resources and disrupted the entire population of the country for years.

The Kings, themselves, might never actually meet on the battlefield. Indeed, they might not even be involved in any actual fighting at all because they could watch from the nearest hill and give orders to the foot soldiers who died on their behalf. A Celtic Kingship fight was a question of personal valour between two contenders, usually resulting in one death at the most. A Kingship struggle in patrilineal society resulted in mass graves dug by the common people for the common people.

Perhaps by the time Meleagant abducted Gwenivere, Arthur had had enough of personal valour. He had fought Pellinore for Lot's wife and lost. He had fought Accolon and almost lost his life through Morgan's trickery, he may well have already rescued Gwenivere once from Melwas and although he still had Excalibur he had forfeited its magical scabbard. When Gwenivere was abducted again Arthur may have thought hard about the advantages which Christianity seemed to offer.

To start with, under Christianity women would not assume such an important role in society nor in his personal life. He would no longer have to worship the Goddess who seemed to be asking so much of him and who was probably so difficult for him to understand. A male God, on his own, without a Goddess might have seemed easier for him to relate to - less mysterious and more straightforward in his dealings with mortal men perhaps.

If women were seen as less important and men could dominate with divine impunity, then Arthur would not have to tread to carefully with the women who had the power to affect his life to much, like Morgan-Le-Fay for instance. Perhaps he was hoping that a new God would offer him protection against female magic and manipulation. If under Christianity he no longer had to depend upon his wife for his position, if his territory was his own and not his wife's, then he would no longer have to worry about her being abducted or the possibility of a young challenger. If someone wanted his Kingdom, from now on it would be army to army not man to man.

This would be much less risky for Arthur as an individual. He would no longer have to summon up the same amount of personal courage and face the loneliness of one to one combat, from which there was no escape without loss of honour and where no-one would rescue you if you should fall. With army facing army a King could lose a battle or even a war and still stand a very good chance of escaping with his life.

To Arthur then, at this point in his career, Christianity must have seemed like a very good idea. Changing over from one religion to another, however, may have been the solution to some of Arthur's problems but it also presented him with a number of others and he could not afford to ignore them. Firstly, if he was turning his back on the Goddess for ever he was obviously running the risk of incurring Her wrath and there was no telling what action She might take against him. Presumably he was at this time taking council from some Christian advisors and they were no doubt telling him that the Goddess would do nothing at all. After all, Christian militants had played a major role in closing down Goddess temples all over Europe and were always actively trying to pursued men to give up Her religion and join theirs. Maybe they were even boasting to Arthur that the Goddess was powerless to act against their God and that She had never done anything in the past when men had forsaken Her. All the same it must have been quite a source of anxiety for him especially since he had already enjoyed so much of Her goodwill.

Secondly, the people who made up his court and the people who lived on the land were all Celts. It would take a long time for them to change over from one way of life to another, and undoubtedly the vast majority of them would be most reluctant to even think about it - especially the people who farmed the land. Remember that it was part of the old religious culture that the King represented the Young God and the Young God ensured that the land would be fertile and the crops would grow. They would not be very willing to risk their livelihoods for the sake of a new religion. Changing people's long standing beliefs is a tricky business and cannot be achieved overnight.

Thirdly, Arthur had a problem with Gwenivere. The people regarded her as the holder of the sovereignty of the land and as a representation of the Goddess. He needed to either change their perception of her or to get rid of her altogether if he wanted to make himself sovereign in his own right. He obviously could not simply kill her outright for he would be risking his own life at the hands of the population and just as obviously it would take a very long time before the Christian missionaries could either convince or coerce everyone to give up their religion and disregard its ways.

Things were further complicated by the fact that under Christianity sovereignty was a male preserve to be passed on from father to son but he and Gwenivere had no children. His only son, Mordred, was illegitimate and therefore did not count in the eyes of the Church. Moreover, the Church, at this time being completely Catholic, did not allow its faithful to divorce so he could not simply re-marry someone else. Arthur was stuck with Gwenivere until he could figure out a way to get rid of her without creating any more problems for himself.

When Meleagant abducted Gwenivere and Arthur announced that he was powerless to do anything about it, he must have been praying to his new God that she would not return to him. Perhaps he was even hoping that she might get killed and so solve his problem altogether. He must have been really upset when Lancelot escorted Gwenivere back to her court unharmed. Clearly things were not going to be very easy for him.

Guinevere

Chapter Seven

In many ways Celtic queens found themselves in an unenviable position. Although they undoubtedly commanded a great deal of respect and power they could never be sure of being wanted or loved for their own sakes. One question must always have been in the back of their minds. "Does this man want me because he loves me or does he want me because I can make him a King?" As far as Gwenivere was concerned it must have been obvious to her at this stage what Arthur's motives towards her were and having been abducted once or maybe even twice she obviously knew why Meleagant and Melwas were interested in her. So what could she expect from Lancelot? Did he really love her or was he too simply interested in becoming the new king of her territory?

This question of whether a man was interested in a woman for the power or position she could bestow on him was a crucial one in a matrilineal society and could even be extended to the Goddess Herself. The Goddess was the ultimate maker and breaker of Kings and She too would want it demonstrated that She was loved and respected for Her own sake rather than being worshipped simply because She could grant so much to an ordinary man. Hence the situation arose then that men were tested in some way or another before they were considered suitable as husbands or kings or, as in the case of the Goddess, before they were considered worthy of receiving Her favours. Sometimes it might have been a simple test of combat, sometimes several more complex situations to endure and win through. This could explain why the Knights in the Arthurian legends were always expected to do extraordinary deeds and why they were so often tempted with other women before they were able to win the hand of the Lady of their choice. A good example of this is the tale of the 'Fair Unknown'.

The earliest surviving account of this story is by the Frenchman Renand de Beaujeu. Its hero is Guinglain, the son of Gawain and a beautiful fay. Guinglain never knew his real name, his mother raised him by herself and simply called him Fair Son. When he came of age he went to Arthur's court to become a knight. There he was sent on a mission to rescue a Welsh Queen known as Blond Esmeree who had been turned into a dragon by two sorcerers. She could only be released from the enchantment by a kiss.

On the way to save the queen, Guinglain was forced to do battle with a number of hostile knights who challenged him and had to rescue several damsels in distress. He came eventually to a place known as the Golden Island where a beautiful fay called La Pucelle lived. She fell in love with Guinglain and wanted him to marry her but he refused and continued his rescue mission. At last he arrived at the town of Senaudon where Blond Esmeree was being held. The town had been turned into a wasteland because of the evil of the two sorcerers.

Guinglain challenged the sorcerers and although they used their magic he was able to overcome them. He then came face to face with a most hideous serpent which demanded to be kissed. Guinglain consented and the serpent changed into the beautiful Esmeree.

Esmeree too wanted to marry Guinglain because he had faced so many dangers on her behalf and had not been afraid of her when she had appeared so hideous. Guinglain agreed to marry her but first wanted to return to Arthur's court for a tournament. On the way he stopped at the Golden Island once more where La Pucelle explained that she had used her magic to help him overcome the two sorcerers. He stayed with her for a while but eventually went back to Camelot and was there re-united with Esmeree. They married and returned to Senandon where the wasteland had come back to life again and he became its new King.

Guinglain had to face many challenges, hardships and temptations before he married and became king, presumably that was in order to make sure that he was worthy of the position. A similar thing happened to Lancelot. Even though he was brought up by the Lady of the Lake herself and could therefore be regarded for all intents and purposes as the son of the Goddess, he too was tested in order to reveal his true intentions. In Lancelot's case, however, he seemed to have been tested to determine whether he was simply interested in Gwenivere for her kingdom or whether he actually loved her.

Morgan Le Fay played a part in these events, once more acting on behalf of the darker side of the Goddess, as it were, in order to create difficulties and situations through which Lancelot could be put to the test. He never became a king but he was offered the chance and he turned it down because of Gwenivere.

In the town of Corbenic lived a very beautiful girl named Elaine. Morgan-Le-Fay put a spell on her which meant that she would be boiled alive in a tub of water unless the best knight in the land could rescue her. Corbenic was the home of the Grail at that particular time and it was being kept in the castle of King Pelles. Lancelot managed to rescue Elaine and then discovered that she was the daughter of Pelles. The lady fell in love with Lancelot and wanted to marry him but he refused. Pelles also wanted Lancelot to marry Elaine and so he persuaded a sorceress to make Elaine resemble Gwenivere and Lancelot was fooled into sleeping with her. Elaine conceived a son whom she named Galahad.

News of all this soon reached Arthur's court and Gwenivere was really upset, until Lancelot explained how he had been tricked. Sometime later, however, Pelles brought Elaine to the court and once again Lancelot was deceived into sleeping with her. This time Gwenivere was inconsolable. She threw Lancelot out of the court and said she never wanted to see him again. Rejected by Gwenivere Lancelot went mad. He took to the forests and lived as a wild man for two years. The other knights searched for him but he was unrecognisable. Eventually he wandered into Corbenic where Elaine realised who he was and took him to the room in the castle where the Grail was kept. The Grail restored him to sanity and he stayed with Elaine for a year, but he greatly missed Gwenivere and was very unhappy. Eventually Sir Hector persuaded him to return to Arthur's court and Gwenivere was delighted to have him back again.

Lancelot had spent a whole year with Elaine, and before that he had spent two years in the forest. Now living as a wild man in the forest has a very special significance in the Celtic world. Merlin was a wild man before he became a master sorcerer. It was an experience closely linked with a magical or shamanic training. A time spent becoming closer to nature and the ways of the Goddess; a time alone away from the distractions of the outside world. It can be no co-incidence that when Lancelot rejoined society once more he was taken into the presence of the Grail. It signifies that he had completed some inner magical journey and was rewarded by the Grail itself. As explained before, the Grail was a beautiful mysterious object special to the Celtic religion and symbolic of the abundance of the Goddess herself. It also lay at the heart of the replacement of the King ceremony whereby the young virile new King took over from the old King and the land was replenished. Pelles wanted Lancelot to marry his daughter. In other words he wanted Lancelot, the best knight in the land, to take over his role as King in Corbenic.

Elaine was obviously the woman who held the sovereignty of this territory and Lancelot could have become its new King. Kingship was not on his mind, however, Gwenivere was and so he gave it all up and returned to her.

Shortly before Lancelot left Corbenic a very sick knight appeared at Arthur's court. He was slowly dying and had been told that only the best knight in the land could save him. Knowing that the best knights were at Arthur's court he had travelled there in the hope that one of them could help. None of the knights at the court, including Arthur, were able to do anything; however, when Lancelot returned the knight was cured.

In Malory's version of events Lancelot prayed to the Christian God to save the knight. Given the fact that Lancelot was the adopted son of the Lady of the Lake, however, this seems highly unlikely. The cure probably had much more to do with the fact that Lancelot was now being favoured by the Goddess and had spent time in the presence of the Grail. Perhaps its regenerative powers had somehow become attached to Lancelot for a while and so he was able to help the knight. Whichever way the cure was effected, Lancelot's position as the best knight in the land would seem to have been confirmed. Only the best knight could save Elaine and only the best knight could help cure the sick stranger.

As the best knight in the land and the Queen's lover besides, Lancelot would surely have been more than a match for Arthur if he had cared to challenge him for the right to be Gwenivere's husband. Lancelot, however, did not push himself forward. Most commentators have assumed that this was because Lancelot was extremely loyal to Arthur as King but perhaps there were other reasons behind his apparent reluctance. For one thing Lancelot was clearly a man of the Goddess. He might, therefore, have been hesitant to act against a man who at one stage at least had enjoyed the Goddess's patronage. Even if Lancelot could be sure that Arthur no longer had the Goddess's favour it is possible that he may have been uncertain as to how the next step should be taken. Arthur had already demonstrated that he was not interested in accepting personal challenges anymore. If he was steadily trying to change his followers into the ways of the Christian religion then Lancelot might well be accused of committing treason against the king instead of proposing a lawful challenge under the Celtic tradition. Arthur might well have had enough supporters of the new ways around him already to seize Lancelot and have him put to death as a traitor. Thus Lancelot would have to tread very carefully.

Morgan-Le-Fay, on the other hand, had no such worries. If Lancelot felt powerless to act then Morgan set out to make sure that the stalemate was broken. In order to force a confrontation between Lancelot and Arthur she began to do her level best to make it clear to Arthur that Gwenivere and Lancelot were lovers. Morgan managed to waylay Lancelot a couple of times. Once when he fell asleep under an apple tree he was spirited away to her castle but managed to escape. On another occasion he was not so lucky and was held prisoner for several months. During his captivity he passed the time by drawing pictures of himself and Gwenivere on the bedroom walls. After he had escaped Morgan invited Arthur to the castle and displayed the artwork to him, after which Arthur became very suspicious of Gwenivere.

Gwenivere had given Lancelot a ring and on one occasion Morgan gave Lancelot a drug to make him sleep and took the ring from his finger. While Lancelot was away from Camelot Morgan sent the ring to the court with a message supposedly from Lancelot which said that he was dying and that he deeply regretted his affair with the Queen. Gwenivere swore that her affection for Lancelot was innocent and Arthur said that he believed her. On another occasion Morgan had a magic vessel sent to the court from which no woman who was unfaithful to her husband could drink. Many women at the court drank from it but Gwenivere refused knowing who it was from.

It Arthur had become a Christian by now things must have been very difficulty indeed for Gwenivere especially at the court. Arthur must have been steadily building up his personal power and influence at the expense of hers, and was backed up in this process by his new religion. Most of Gwenivere's power was derived from the fact that she was regarded as a representation of the Mother Goddess and as such held to be sovereign over the land. As the influence of Christianity gradually took hold around the court the notion that the Divine being was male rather than female would be gaining ground and alongside this the parallel idea that sovereignty belonged to men and not women would be gradually creeping into men's minds. Eventually then the influence of and respect for the Queen must have gradually begun to diminish as their ideals and values changed from one system of religion to the other. As her power and influence began to wane, Gwenivere would have had to tread very carefully at the court and probably often feared for her life as well as for the life of Lancelot her lover. One very good reason indeed for denying her affair with him so vehemently.

Arthur too must have been in a very delicate position trying to change over from one system or religion to another. He would have had to feel his way very carefully not knowing how far he could push the new ideas and standards because the people in the court and the people on the land were used to the old Celtic ways. If he had tried to change things too quickly there would have been the danger of stirring up resentments or even rebellion against himself. He would not have been sure whether people would be loyal to him as King or loyal to the Queen as the Celtic sovereign. It must have been obvious to him for a very long time that Lancelot and Gwenivere were lovers but to acknowledge the affair publicly could have brought great difficulties.

Under Christianity adultery was a grave sin which a Queen especially should not indulge in and which merited some form of punishment. While Arthur was still unsure of his own position, he could not afford to run the risk of trying to punish her in any way in case the court and the ordinary people did not approve. This was because under Celtic tradition adultery by the Queen was seen as a fairly common prelude to getting rid of the old King and would normally end in a personal challenge to the old King. This would have been something that Arthur would be determined to avoid at all costs just in case he lost. After all, he could no longer have expected the Goddess to help him fight a personal challenge like this anymore because by now he had well and truly turned his back upon Her. On the other hand, he could hardly have expected his new Christian God to help him either because this kind of particular contest belonged completely to the traditions established by a religion which Christianity was so determined to stamp out.

For many years, then, Arthur was stuck between a rock and a hard place (as the saying goes); too afraid to acknowledge the affair between Lancelot and Gwenivere because of the possible consequences. He would have needed to be totally certain that he had enough support for the new ways before he had the confidence to take any kind of action against Gwenivere and Lancelot.

Meanwhile, Arthur had other problems on his mind. Something was happening to the kingdom. It was as if a spell had been cast over the land. Arthur's kingdom, once so fertile and prosperous was slowly being transformed into a dark and barren wasteland.

In an early Grail story known as the *'Didot Perceval'*, the unknown author hints that this wasting of the land was somehow brought about by Perceval himself. There was a seat at the Round Table that was always left empty. It was known as the 'Siege Perilous' and reserved for the hero who was meant to win the Grail.

Perceval sat in this seat one day and immediately it split into two with a terrible sound and from the ground beneath the seat a thick shadowy cloud arose. From within the cloud a voice declared that the enchantment of Britain would not end until the best knight in the world came to the house of the Fisher King and asked the question "What is done with the Grail and whom does it serve?".

Another French Grail romance, this time the 13th Century story known as *Perlesvaus*, also implies that the condition of the land was somehow the fault of the hero. Perlesvaus had already found the Grail castle once but had failed to ask the crucial question "Whom does it serve?" and because of this all kinds of evil befell the kingdom.

The Fisher King himself was struck by disease, Perlesvaus fell ill, King Arthur slipped into a state of total apathy and all the knights deserted him. The Kingdom was ravaged by war and worse still, according to the author, "the progress of Christianity, whose triumph over Jews, Muslims and Pagans is the principle duty of Arthur and his champions has been greatly impeded".

Apparently, if Perlesvaus had asked the question of the Grail he would have shown himself to be the next rightful King but as it was the Fisher King did not recognise him.

An evil King took Perlesvaus' place and in the end Perlesvaus had to seize the castle back by force. When he did so the enchantment of the land was lifted.

In Malory's version of events the Grail hero was Galahad. In his story he follows closely the French *'Queste del Saint Graal'* which appeared in the *Vulgate Cycle* of Arthurian Legend. As mentioned before, the Vulgate Cycle is believed to have been written by Cistercian monks who used it as a way of spreading their own propaganda. They were extremely influential in the early 13th Century and they clearly wanted to distance the ever popular Arthurian tales from their Celtic/Goddess origins as much as possible.

In both *Perceval* and *Perlesvaus,* the hero who won the Grail quest was meant to become the next King, taking over the position of the old maimed King. This of course clearly reflects the Celtic tradition of replacing the old King and thereby replenishing the land. Even though both of those stories have been Christianised and the Grail itself described as the "Holy Grail" with all the obvious Christian connotations, the main purpose of the quest was still to ask the all important question "Whom does it serve?". Only by asking this question was the special chain of events set in motion whereby the old maimed King was restored to health and the bewitched wasteland became once again more fertile.

The authors of the *'Queste del Saint Graal'* must have realised that the Celtic origins of these stories were still very recognisable and decided to try to Christianise the story completely in order to remove from it all traces of the Goddess religion. In order to do this they first invented a new Grail hero - Galahad. Galahad was the perfect knight. He had no failings whatsoever and he never had anything to do with women at all (obviously not a man of the Goddess, unlike his father Lancelot). When Galahad found the Grail he no longer had to ask "Who does it serve?" instead the Grail has been elevated to a kind of beatific vision which was now granted only to the worthy and by the 'grace of God'.

Galahad was introduced to the court one day by an old man who appeared suddenly from nowhere. The old man announced that Galahad was the champion who would break the spell on the land and led him to sit in the 'Siege Perilous'. Unlike the story about Perceval nothing happened when he sat in the seat, but sometime later all the assembled court saw a vision of the Grail and were struck dumb. When speech was returned to them Gawain immediately declared that he would go in search of the Grail and not return before he found it.

Lancelot, Perceval and all the other knights also swore to find out the truth about the Grail and everyone, apart from Arthur and the ladies of the court (who were apparently not allowed to venture after the Holy Grail), set out on the quest. The Grail castle was almost impossible to locate because it regularly disappeared and reappeared in different places so most of the knights eventually arrived back at the court without even seeing it. Lancelot glimpsed it at a distance but was immediately knocked out by the sight of it and had to return. Galahad, Perceval and Bors joined forces and eventually after many adventures discovered its whereabouts. They were welcomed inside by King Pelles and a mysterious voice invited them to sit at the table of Jesus Christ and eat the food of heaven. The old maimed King was carried in and then the Holy Grail accompanied by the Lance of

Longinus brought in by Angels. Blood flowed from the tip of the lance into the Grail and then Jesus appeared and gave them all communion. He told them that the Grail must leave Britain because its people were too sinful and worldly but the spell on the land would be lifted anyway.

Jesus then disappeared and Galahad took some blood from the lance and touched the leg of the maimed King who was immediately healed. The three knights then took the Grail by ship to Jerusalem where, one year later, Galahad was allowed to look into the Grail itself. Its innermost secrets were then revealed to him and it so overwhelmed him that he no longer desired to live on this Earth. His soul was taken straight to Heaven and the Grail and the Lance disappeared into the sky. In Britain the spell on the land was broken and was restored once more to its normal fertile state.

In the previous Grail stories then the hero who obtained the Grail and restored the land was meant to replace the old king and become King himself as long as he asked the right question. In the 'Queste del Saint Graal' however, and in Malory's version, Galahad obtained the restoration of the land by the 'Grace of God' and did so on behalf of Arthur and his Kingdom. Galahad did not replace the old King but instead died himself and ascended to Heaven. Obviously, this was a deliberate attempt by the Cistercian monks to disassociate the Grail from the traditional Celtic change of Kingship ceremony which normally accompanied the Grail quest. This time the hero himself died, or is sacrificed - rather like Jesus, and the old King, as represented by Arthur lived on. the Grail was then lost to the world for ever because the people of Britain were too sinful and no longer worthy of its presence.

Thus the Grail, one of the last remaining important symbols of the religion of the Goddess, was taken away from the world by the hand of the male Christian God. Presumably, these Cistercian monks hoped that along with it all remaining traces of the Goddess religion in Britain would disappear as well. Perhaps they were also hoping too that no-one would bother to think of searching for the Grail anymore now that it was safely in the hands of their God. They even replaced the women Grail bearers by Angels!

None of these Christianised versions of the Grail quest fully explained what exactly happened to the land in Arthur's kingdom; we are simply told that the land was laid waste by a spell or bewitchment. Perceval and Perlesvaus hinted that it was all the fault of the hero himself, while the 'Queste' and Malory suggest that it was because of the immoral behaviour of the people who were too sinful and worldly, particularly Lancelot and Gwenivere. This was of course why Lancelot was not fit to see the Holy Grail. He could only glimpse the castle as a distance and even then it knocked him unconscious.

It seems to have been forgotten that Lancelot had already been in the presence of the Grail itself and far from knocking him out it had restored his sanity! He also seems to have been replaced as the best knight in the land by his own son, Galahad, which is of course a none too subtle hint at the supposed superiority of patrilineal succession.

If we turn to Celtic tradition, however, there is a much more convincing explanation for the barrenness of Arthur's kingdom. It happened because Arthur was simply no longer fit to be King. In the Goddess religion the King was meant to represent the young-God who guaranteed the fertility of the land by his own death and rebirth - but Arthur had turned his back upon the Goddess and Her religion! He was no longer willing to put his ability or fitness to rule to the test. He was no longer willing to accept lawful challenges. If he had accepted Meleagant's challenge and won he would have proved himself still an able and virile King, fit to rule and worthy of representing the Young God.

By shunning the Celtic ways in favour of the new Christianity Arthur was demonstrating to the world that he was no longer fit to rule. He was demonstrating that he was far more interested in being a King for the sake of the power and prestige the position offered him than in being a good leader who was concerned about his people and the state of the land they depended upon. In other words, Arthur was far more concerned about himself than about his people and had outlived his usefulness as an appropriate leader, so the Goddess watched as his kingdom turned into a wasteland.

Christian commentators have always viewed the female sex with the greatest suspicion ever since their religion was invented. They see most women as semi-witches capable of casting spells and enchanting men. Thus when the greatest female of all, the Mother of Creation Herself, withdraws her support from the land as a mark of her displeasure with Arthur they could only think to describe it as an enchantment or spell that had been cast over Britain. And yet, if Arthur had still been fit to be King this wasting of the land would never have occurred. It was a sign for all to see that it was time for the old King to be replaced.

Lancelot was the obvious candidate to be the new King. He was spiritually in tune with the Goddess and the land, he had obtained the Grail many years before and he was accepted by Gwenivere as a suitable lover. Arthur, however, would not acknowledge his right as a lawful challenger. Arthur wanted to change the rules. He required a new champion, someone who could obtain the Grail on his behalf and replenish the land without Arthur himself being replaced. So Sir Galahad, the innocent virgin, was sacrificed in Arthur's place. Instead of the King dying to save the land one of his servants was chosen instead so that Arthur could continue his rule. No wonder he was not fit to be King anymore and the land had gone to waste. The noble element of self sacrifice, or at least a willingness to be put to the test, had completely left him.

By turning to Christianity Arthur had hoped to remain King at the same time avoiding his responsibility as custodian of the land. He wanted his new God to take on the Goddess and so save him from having to prove himself still worthy of being a leader. The Cistercian monks understood this only too well. They had their God take away the Grail forever and restore the land without the necessity of replacing the old King. By this act they were declaring that in future, Kings would no longer have to worry about old customs for the condition of the land was no longer their responsibility. They could now leave it all up to the new God who would replenish the land, regardless of how they acted or what they did. By making the Grail disappear into the sky perhaps they were hoping that they could make the Goddess disappear also. It was a symbolic way of saying that Christianity had finally triumphed over the Goddess in Britain.

When the land of Britain was returned to fertility once more and Arthur was still in place as King he must have been rejoicing and he probably convinced himself that he was free of the Goddess for ever. The Goddess, however, had not yet quite finished with him!

Chapter Eight

After the enchantment on the land of Britain had been lifted and Arthur was still able to call himself King he must have begun to feel a little more secure about his future. With the help of his new religion he had survived the wasteland. He had neither been replaced by a new King nor did he have to go through the ordeal of proving himself worthy to continue his reign. Arthur probably took this as a sign that the Christian God was now on his side and looking after him. Perhaps it was now time to take care of the other pressing problem on his mind - what to do about Gwenivere. As long as she was alive Gwenivere would always pose a threat to his ambition to claim the sovereignty of Britain as his very own. As long as she remained Queen there would always be some who would regard her as sovereign rather than himself.

It must have been obvious to the people around the court at least that all was not well between Gwenivere and Arthur. The Queen was still involved in her long-standing affair with Lancelot and this must by now have been common knowledge to everyone even if Arthur himself was still refusing to acknowledge it. Arthur, for his part, had long ago demonstrated his feelings towards the Queen when he refused to lift a finger to rescue her from the clutches of Meleagant and, before long, when Gwenivere was once again in dire need of support and assistance, it was not her husband Arthur who provided it.

According to Malory, someone at the court had a grudge against Gawain and prepared a poisoned apple for him. Unknowingly, the Queen passed this poisoned apple to another knight who died almost as soon as he had eaten it. Everyone immediately suspected Gwenivere of murder and to prove that she was innocent she had to find a champion to fight on her behalf. Unfortunately for Gwenivere she had temporarily fallen out with Lancelot because she had suspected him of being unfaithful again and he had left the court several days before.

The charge of murder was a serious one and carried the death penalty even for a sovereign but no knight in the court would stand as her champion especially not her husband, Arthur. Luckily for Gwenivere however, news of her plight reached Lancelot and he returned to Camelot incognito to stand on her behalf. He was still the best Knight in the land and was able to win the contest easily, thus proving Gwenivere's innocence. They made up their quarrel and soon became lovers once again. This time, however, people at the court began talking about them and suddenly Arthur began taking notice of the gossip. He decided to set a trap to catch the lovers together.

We must ask ourselves the question why did Arthur suddenly decide that the rumours might be true after all? Why only now, after all these years, did he plan to find out once and for all if his wife really was having an affair with Lancelot? The answer can only be that the incident with the poisoned apple demonstrated clearly to him that

Gwenivere was no longer being held in such high esteem by the members of the court. Not one of the knights would stand up for her. Maybe now then he could act with confidence against her. The years of 'behind the scenes' persuasion and Christian propaganda had at last begun to pay off.

The minds of those closest to him were being turned in his favour, after all he had survived the wasteland. The power of the Goddess must have seemed to be on the wane and the new God had apparently removed the Grail for ever. The old loyalties were obviously beginning to weaken and Arthur must have judged that the time was now right to move against his Queen. With luck he could be rid of both her and Lancelot in one fell swoop.

Early one morning the trap was sprung. Lancelot and Gwenivere were discovered in bed together. The Lady of the Lake must have been on Lancelot's side that morning for he managed to escape. Gwenivere, however, was not so fortunate. She was taken captive and immediately sentenced to death by her ever-loving and all-forgiving Christian husband. She was to be burnt alive! News of the events quickly spread to the town and the villages. The people were outraged because as far as they were concerned Gwenivere was still their sovereign. They became very restive but plans for the execution went ahead nevertheless.

Lancelot hurriedly gathered together a small force of men and rode towards the place of execution. He arrived in the nick of time just seconds before Gwenivere was about to be burnt to death. A terrible fight took place and many of Arthur's men were killed, including two of his nephews. These knights had been Lancelot's friends and this troubled him deeply but he was able to rescue Gwenivere and took her away to safety. Soon after, civil war broke out between the followers of Lancelot and the followers of Arthur. In the heat of battle Lancelot had the opportunity to kill Arthur when he was not looking, but being a knight of honour he refused to put an end to him in such an ignominious manner.

As a man of the Goddess no doubt Lancelot would have preferred, even at this stage, the more traditional one to one combat situation. True to form, however, Arthur denied Lancelot his chance of an honourable revenge and seized the opportunity to turn the battle into a siege instead. The siege went on for months until a message arrived form the Pope in Rome ordering Arthur to forgive Gwenivere and take her back as his wife once more. So Arthur offered to lift the siege and forget the feud against Lancelot on condition that Gwenivere returned to him. Gwenivere eventually agreed to the terms and Lancelot was allowed to leave for France.

This apparent move towards reconciliation quite obviously did not come about as a result of a change of heart in either Arthur or Gwenivere for they must have really loathed each other by now. It was obviously more a question of expediency on both their parts. As a supposedly committed Christian, Arthur could not afford to displease the head of his new church. He might well need the Pope's support in future. As for Gwenivere, she must have been taking a gamble that Arthur would feel compelled to keep his word to the Pope and not have either herself or Lancelot killed if she surrendered.

If the siege had been in force for many months they probably would have starved to death very soon anyway.

At least if they were still alive there was always the chance that Gwenivere and Lancelot might be reunited in the future. Arthur, however, soon proved that he was not to be trusted. Once he had Gwenivere back he immediately followed Lancelot to France with the intention of seeing him dead, even if it was not by his own hands He persuaded Gawain to challenge Lancelot in fair combat and lent him Excalibur in order to improve his chances of winning. Although the two had been friends for many years and had shared many adventures together, Lancelot had killed Gawain's brothers while rescuing Gwenivere and Gawain was out for revenge.

Lancelot was reluctant to fight but Gawain insisted. Even with Excalibur however, Gawain was no match for Lancelot and was soon defeated. Lancelot begged him to yield but he refused. Lancelot though could not bring himself to kill his old comrade even if his comrade wanted to kill him, so he sheathed his sword and walked away.

Before Arthur had time to work out how he could rid himself of Lancelot, news arrived from Britain which forced him to return swiftly. He had left Gwenivere in the custody of his son Mordred, who had assured him that he would look after her. Mordred, however, had his own reasons for offering this service. As soon as Arthur was safely in France Mordred arranged for a letter to be sent to the court claiming that Arthur had been killed by Lancelot. The letter said that on his deathbed Arthur had declared Mordred should be the next King and should marry Gwenivere. Gwenivere was completely opposed to this idea but she was by now Mordred's captive and he began to attract many supporters.

By the time Arthur returned to Britain, Mordred had raised an army to stand against him. Father and son finally faced each other across the lush meadows of their Cornish homeland. Here, on the banks of the river Camel at a place known as Camlan, Arthur's final battle began. On that day Mordred was killed by his own father and Arthur was killed by his own son.

The Christian interpretation of the legends more or less suggested that Arthur met his death in this manner as a kind of punishment from the Christian God because his son was not only born out of wedlock but was also the result of an incestuous relationship (even if Arthur supposedly did not know at the time). However, these events, looked at from the Celtic view point demonstrate that Arthur's demise was in fact the final irony. The man who used the Goddess to become King and then turned his back upon Her and matrilineal succession in an attempt to secure for himself the advantages that patrilinear succession seemed to offer, was forced in the end to kill his own son and in turn his son dealt him a fateful blow.

Far from being an act of punishment from the Christian God it was in reality a fitting act of revenge on the part of the Goddess. On that fateful day the Goddess made sure that for Arthur at least the notion of patrilinear succession was totally meaningless. Never would Arthur or his male line reap any advantages through being so treacherous.

Mordred had made a bid for Arthur's kingship but he did not do so under the rules of patrilineal succession for Mordred was illegitimate and thus not a legal heir. The only way Mordred could be King was by matrilineal succession. He had to marry the Queen, he had to revert to Celtic tradition and when Gwenivere refused to marry him he abducted her. Arthur had never been open to challenges in the Celtic way but at last he was forced to fight for his kingship and his challenger was no less than his own son! Arthur had tried to change the system but in his final hours he had been totally outmanoeuvred and the Goddess took her revenge.

As Arthur lay dying on the battlefield he must have realised finally the terrible mistake he had made. He should never have turned his back upon the Goddess, the most powerful being in the universe. He had sought honour and glory for himself alone but in doing so he had merely managed to bring about his own destruction. In the closing minutes of his life his final act was not the act of a Christian King. He did not seek to find peace with his Christian God, he did not ask for a Priest to give him the last rites or a final Blessing, instead he sought to placate the Goddess. He ordered his last remaining knight, Bedivere, to return Excalibur to the lake from whence it came.

Bedivere refused at first. He must have thought that Arthur had gone mad. After all, he must have been talking about the virtues of his new religion for years by now and no doubt had tried hard to pursued everyone at the court to join him. But Arthur was serious; he insisted that Bedivere should follow his instructions. So the knight took Excalibur to the nearby lake and threw it high over the water. Before Excalibur could touch the surface an arm rose from beneath the lake and caught it. The hand shook the sword three times and then vanished beneath the surface once more taking Excalibur with it. Three was the mystic number of the Celts and a sign for all to see that the sword had been returned to the

Goddess. The Lady of the Lake had taken back that which she had given and soon after Arthur died.

Returning Excalibur to the lake was a final admission on Arthur's part that he had been wrong. At the very end of his life he had been forced to acknowledge the power of the Goddess and Her superiority over his new male God. According to the legend Arthur's body was not given a Christian burial he was simply carried away by the Lady of the Lake and Morgan-Le-Fay in a boat bound for Avalon.

Some people like to believe that this was specially arranged so that he could be healed and brought back to life again at some future time. After the treachery he had shown towards the Goddess and Her religion, however, it hardly seems likely that She would be happy to let him live again. Surely he caused enough trouble in one lifetime! No, it seems more likely that they took him to Avalon because that is where Morgan-Le-Fay's castle was to be found guarding the entrance to the otherworld. No doubt Arthur still lies there now, eternally imprisoned somewhere in the dark depths of that otherworld.

Does he really deserve any other fate?

Conclusions

For many centuries the legend of King Arthur has remained an enigma, stimulating the imagination of generations of Arthurian addicts. Literally scores of books have been written on this subject, the vast majority of which are mostly concerned about whether Arthur really existed. If so where was he born? Where was the fabled town of Camelot? Where was he actually buried? And so on. This theme is still being played out. Only recently another book has been added to the collection. Entitled 'Arthur the True Story', the authors Philips and Keatman, claim to have discovered that the name Arthur stands for the word 'Bear' in the old language and that this was really a title rather than a man's name.

This is all very interesting but hardly a new discovery since Richard Cavendish pointed out the connection between the name Arthur and the old word for bear as long ago as 1978, while Nicholas Gold makes repeated use of the "name equals title" theory in his book 'The Queen and the Cauldron'. Disregarding these discrepancies however, the important point about this latest publication is that Philips and Keatman claim that Arthur's real

name was probably Owain Ddantgwyn, a Celtic King from the Shropshire region and that he had no connection at all with either Tintagel or Glastonbury.

Tintagel is apparently ruled out because the existing castle was built in the 12th Century by a son of Henry 1 and before that there had been a monastery on the same site. They conclude that he could not have been born in the castle because it obviously was not built at the time and that he was unlikely to have been born in a monastery.

Now this may seem like a fair enough assumption on the surface perhaps but such a cursory analysis of the situation is hardly sufficient to warrant the dismissal of such a long standing traditional association. Surely it deserves a little more thought than this! After all, Geoffrey of Monmouth, who first placed Arthur's birth at Tintagel, was some 850 years closer to the time of his birth than we are today and therefore much nearer to those original Celtic sources. If those sources placed Arthur's birth at Tintagel why should anyone want to disagree?

Legends and stories do not generally materialise out of thin air, there is usually some basis of truth to be found in them and the Celtic bards were not exactly in the pay of the Cornish tourist board at the time.

Geoffrey's '*History*' was published in 1135, the same century that the present castle (now in ruins) was built so presumably he did realise that Arthur could not have been born in this particular building. The fact that the ruins which existed before the castle were once part of a monastery however, does not rule out the possibility that

Arthur was born there. A building could be a Celtic stronghold in one century and a cowshed in another - the one use does not preclude the other.

In a similarly superficial manner Philips and Keatman also rule out the possibility that Arthur was buried in Glastonbury. They arrive at this conclusion because (as we pointed out early on in this book) the monks who claim to have discovered his remains near the Abbey were out for publicity at the time and apparently were also after new funds to build a bigger and better Abbey. Is this sufficient enough reason to throw out the Glastonbury connection completely? After all, the Abbey is not the only ancient site in the Glastonbury area where he could have been buried. Remember that in the legend Arthur is taken away by two decidedly un-Christian characters - the Lady of the Lake and Morgan-Le-Fay. If these two disposed of his body it hardly seems likely that they took him to the Abbey for a Christian send off!

In view of the long standing association of Arthur with both Tintagel and Glastonbury, surely it makes more sense to dig a little deeper in to the mystery surrounding the stories instead of rushing to write off the connections completely on the basis of a cursory survey of the evidence. There is a very important factor here which must be taken into consideration before we can have any meaningful discussion about Arthur's birth place. The Christian church went to great lengths to try to cover up or destroy all traces of the Great religion that preceded it. It is a well known historical fact that the early Christians erected new religious buildings on ground previously used by worshippers of the Goddess. How many people are aware, for instance, that St Paul's Cathedral was erected on top of a temple that was once dedicated to the Goddess as Diana? The British countryside is littered with churches built on hill tops where once the Goddess was worshipped. A lot of these churches are dedicated to St Michael, the archangel who was supposed to have thrown the great dragon out of heaven. Students of Christian mythology will know that the dragon is a symbolic representation of the Goddess so a church dedicated to St Michael is obviously meant to protect or seal a site against the power of the Old Religion.

Consider, for example, the little church of St Michael that sits perched upon the top of Glastonbury Tor. Was this really the most convenient place for the local congregation to worship? Hardly, for as anyone who has visited the Tor will realise, it is accessible only to the most able bodied. The legends suggest that Glastonbury Tor was an entrance to the Celtic 'otherworld' and the home of Morgan-Le-Fay. Could this then be the real reason why they chose to build a church in such a strange place? An attempt to neutralise what they perceived as 'evil forces'? It is interesting to note in this connection that the present building is mostly ruined now and that it was erected to replace an earlier church that had been destroyed by an earthquake. Now Britain is not renown for its earthquakes so maybe some places are simply not meant to have Christian buildings on them especially those which might be an entrance to the Celtic 'otherworld'.

If Arthur was taken to Glastonbury to be buried it seems far more likely that he was brought here to the Tor than to the Abbey. Perhaps Philips and Keatman should look to the Tor for his bones rather than some long barrow in Shropshire.

The early Christian church was much closer in time to the Old Religion than we are today and they had a healthy respect for its power. Above all they were terrified that it might make a comeback and they saw it as their duty to obliterate all traces of it wherever possible. They were not always able to achieve this at the sites where the Goddess was actually worshipped because they could not afford to upset the local people too much. For a long time they were forced to incorporate aspects of the Old Religion into the new Christianity. For instance local Goddess names were adopted by the Church and given the status of Sainthood. Thus the Goddess as Brigit became known as St Bridget and Annis became St Anne and so on. It was hoped that by this ploy the locals would be fooled into using the new church buildings and then gradually these 'pagan' aspects could be abandoned as the people became accustomed to the new ways. This is of course one of the reasons why early Celtic Christianity differs so dramatically from the continental variety.

This softly, softly approach would not have been necessary for the fort at Tintagel however. It was not a place of worship as such but just a place full of memories of the old Celtic ways and of magical happenings. If Arthur was born there and the early Christian church knew about it (as indeed they must have done), then it is not outside the realm of possibility that they decided to take over the site and completely 'cleanse' it of its connections to the past. After all, if they knew that Arthur had been born there then they would have realised that his sister Morgan-Le-Fay was also born there and moreover, if Camelot was in the vicinity there was always the possibility that somewhere nearby, trapped in an underground ice-cavern, lay the undead body of Merlin the Magician.

Clearly then, they would need to seal this site very securely indeed against the presence of such powerful 'pagan' forces. It is very possible that the clergy decided to obliterate all traces of the original occupation before they erected their new monastic building. If so then a cursory archaeological survey, such as the one that has been carried out at Tintagel, is unlikely to reveal anything more than mere monastic ruins. They rest would have already been removed or cleverly concealed by the terrified clergy. To dismiss out of hand then Tintagel as Arthur's birthplace and Glastonbury as the place of his burial not only flies in the face of long established tradition it also flies in the face of critical consideration which is perhaps far worse.

In any case, to reduce the legend of Arthur to the level of endless discussions about what his real name might have been and where or where not he might have been born or buried is really to miss the whole point of it all. The real significance of Arthur, the real reason why the stories have endured for so long and intrigued us all for so many centuries is that Arthur's legend is no less than the hidden story of a struggle for dominance of one religion over another and this struggle is played out in the form of one man's life. It is the story of how Arthur, King of Britain abandoned the ancient religion of the Goddess in favour of Christianity in the belief that it would enhance his power and prestige in the world.

In this sense, the story of Arthur represents the story of all of those men who wanted to shake off the Goddess and seek greatness for themselves in the religion of a male God - a religion which probably made them feel more secure and afforded many of them more opportunities for personal advancement. These opportunities for advancement however were only to be won at the expense of women for the new religion entailed the destruction of the old stable social system of matrilineal succession. This system, a natural development arising from the worship of the Goddess, was one in which women were held in high regard. All this was abandoned in favour of patrilineal succession which was a founding principle of the new Christianity.

Throughout Europe the might of the newly Christianised Roman Empire had succeeded in crushing the religion of the Goddess. In Britain however, this ancient religion not only managed to survive but was actually growing stronger as the Celts reasserted themselves - until, that is, the betrayal of Arthur. Arthur used the Goddess and Her tradition in order to establish himself as King and then, once in power, he turned his back upon Her and embraced Christianity instead for only Christianity offered him sovereignty in his own right. The true identity of Arthur is not really that important because the legend of Arthur, the story of his betrayal, represents the betrayal of many men.

Many Celtic leaders must have forsaken the Goddess and the old ways at this crucial time in Britain's history. This religion and the way of life that went with it had served them well for thousands of years but in the end they were seduced by Christianity. They threw it all away without a thought for the Goddess who was their Mother just for the chance of increasing their own personal power and prestige. They threw it all away without a thought for the consequences which would inevitably follow such a decision - the consequences to the land.

Arthur and the Celts succeeded in pushing back the invading hordes of Saxons but the victory proved temporary and hollow. Fifty or sixty years after the estimated time of Arthur's death Britain was overrun completely and the Celts were relegated to the sidelines of history for ever. They survived in the extreme corners of the West, in Wales, Scotland and in Ireland but the language of the land was changed to Anglo-Saxon and the barbarians adopted Christianity.

Arthur stands as a symbol of all those men who made the choice to abandon the old ways, all those Celts who turned their backs on the Goddess to seek power through the male line. When they abandoned Her they not only threw away their religion they also brought ruin upon their own kind and lost forever the largest part of their ancestral lands. No wonder those great Celtic heroes were hardly remembered. The Celts were probably too ashamed to speak of them for centuries! No wonder that in time Arthur came to represent a great English Christian King. If it was not for Arthur and those like him there may never have been any English Christian Kings at all. Britain might well have been the spearhead of a revival of the Old Religion and the land would still be Celtic.

It took five hundred years for the stories about Arthur and his heroes to filter through into the general population and by that time Britain had changed almost beyond recognition. It suffered the invasions of the Angles, the Saxons and the Jutes. It was further battered by the Vikings and then finally it succumbed to the Normans. (All this turmoil - all this rich history - and yet, as far as millions of British school children are taught, nothing happened here before 1066!).

During these five hundred years Christianity tightened its grip on society and came to dominate it completely. As it grew stronger it went to great lengths to try to destroy or conceal all traces of the Old Religion which had been its rival and which the clerics greatly feared might make a come back if they were not vigilant enough in their task of suppression. When the tales of King Arthur and the Grail were at last committed to paper and it was abundantly clear from the outset that they were so tremendously popular, the Church must have been really alarmed. Elements of the Old Religion were easily discernible, especially in the stories of the Grail with its symbolic replacement of the King ceremony which was quite distinctive. If the Clergy could recognise the Old Religion it surely would not be long before the ordinary people would recognise it too and perhaps demand a restoration of the Goddess and the old ways.

Obviously the church could not allow this to happen for it was well aware that the need to worship Divinity as female was never far from the hearts and minds of ordinary people. This is why the Roman Catholic Church had and still does have such a problem with its concept of the 'Virgin Mary'. To millions of people Mary is literally the 'Mother of God' and as such plays a far more important role in the religious lives of ordinary worshippers than the divine male principle that Jesus was meant to represent. The Madonna and Child notion is uncomfortably close to the Goddess and Her son/consort who died and was reborn. Mary has become a substitute Goddess revered the world over and Catholicism is powerless to stop this adoration for to do so would seriously jeopardise the hold they have on the population of so many countries.

It can be no coincidence, that when ordinary Catholics receive 'divine revelations' what they invariably see is a vision of the Virgin Mary rather than a vision of Jesus. One has only to stop to think about the famous visions which have occurred in modern times, such as 'Our Lady of Lourdes' or the visions of Fatima, and consider the interest and excitement these have aroused in people. The places where these events occurred are now holy places of pilgrimage and attract millions every year much to the annoyance of the orthodox Catholic hierarchy. Consider too, the continuing existence of the so called 'Black Madonna's' which are found in Churches throughout Europe and on the South American continent. The church has no official explanation to account for these statues which are held sacred by the local people and paraded through the streets on special occasions. The need for a Divine female presence to worship and adore is obviously still amongst us.

This fact should not really surprise us however, when we consider exactly how many thousands of years the human race has spent in worshipping the Goddess. Twenty-five thousand years is a very long time. The worship of the Goddess is more than a part of our history, it is part of our collective subconsciousness by now and a few thousand years of suppression by a rival male dominated religion has not and will not wipe it out.

Thus, when the stories of Arthur were finally written down and became so popular in such a comparatively short space of time the Christian church almost fell over itself to try to Christianise them before they could be recognised for what they were - tales form a time when there were two religions in the land, not one. They were obviously terrified that the Goddess religion would return so they did their best to disguise and alter the stories so the average reader (or listener) would not recognise the truth.

In some respects their task had been made a little easier. Five hundred years of repression ensured that when the stories began to resurface they were not exactly explicit - they could not afford to be. The Church had such a grip on the country that to write or talk openly about the worship of the Goddess or the theories of regeneration would probably have brought the death sentence down on the head of any Celtic bard foolish enough to do so. No; the stories had to be suitably disguised and enigmatic enough to pass clerical censorship while at the same time recognisable to those who had any knowledge of the old ways and intriguing enough to arouse the curiosity of those who knew nothing of days gone by. The legends of Arthur posed a subtle yet powerful threat to the male dominated Christian religion and so the Christian scribes quickly took out their quills and started scribbling. Before long they had changed the Grail from a symbol of the regenerative power of the Goddess into the Holy Grail, the cup of Jesus. A symbolic gesture in itself perhaps but one which underlines the terrible consequences which have resulted from the abandonment of the Old Religion.

The Goddess was known and worshipped as the Creatress of all things. By Her hand alone we experienced birth, life, death and regeneration. The question "Whom does it serve?" was the key to unlocking that great power. It set the regeneration process in motion. The traditional 'replacement of the King' ceremony was a constant reminder that the land had to be looked after by leaders who understood its needs and who cared about its continual fruitfulness, because if they showed themselves to be inadequate leaders or interested solely in their own personal gain then they could be easily and legally replaced by more suitable candidates. Once the Grail was no longer seen as a symbol of the regenerative power of the Goddess and was transformed by Christianity into the Holy Grail instead it was then taken away from the land of Britain by the hand of the male God. This was a sign that things had changed. It was a sign that the leaders of Britain no longer needed to feel any responsibility for the state of the land.

In the Old Religion, the fertility of the land was dependant upon the King representing the young God. This was a symbol of the joint responsibility that they assumed with the Goddess for the care of the land. The leaders or Kings had to be mindful of the Goddess and Her ways. To remain as leaders they had to be willing to prove their suitability periodically or relinquish their position. They had a personal responsibility within the whole process of renewal. It was a contract between the people and the Goddess. If they played their part then the Goddess played Hers and the land flourished.

When the legend was altered and the Grail became the Holy Grail, the Christian God was deemed to be totally responsible for the state of the land and the leaders of the people were no longer required to provide evidence of worthiness. They could rule continually whether or not they were suitable custodians and leaders and what is more, they could pass on their exalted position to their sons regardless of whether or not they were suitable. They no longer had a duty towards the land itself.

In other words, the way had become clear to exploit the land and its resources for their own personal gain without having to feel any responsibility towards it. They were free to do almost exactly as they liked, to rule exactly as they wanted to without fear of being replaced periodically under the law and without having to fear whether the land would suffer as a consequence because the care of the land was now officially in the hands of God above and nothing whatsoever to do with them.

This divorce of responsibility for the land was a major consequence of the advent of Christianity. It had happened all over Europe and the Middle East but its final act was played out in Britain and it is all recorded in the legend of Arthur. It is no coincidence that the spawning place of the modern wasteland took place in Britain. The industrial revolution was master minded by men who used the land and its precious resources purely for their own monetary gain. These were men who had no feeling of responsibility for what they were doing. All over Britain they threw the peasants off the land and enclosed it, committing huge areas of the country to intensive agriculture for the first time ever. The dispossessed were forced into towns in large numbers to become industrial fodder for the new heavy industries and so the modern wasteland was begun. The only governing factor for the new 'Kings' was to make as much money as possible for themselves and pass on this new wealth to their sons. The good of the land and the good of the people was no longer any concern of theirs.

When the Goddess religion was abandoned men were free to rape the earth and allow its children to perish in the process. The earth was no longer a scared living being, it became an inanimate object. A thing to be used and exploited without fear of the consequences. Animals, plants and minerals, once considered an integral part of the sacred whole and respectfully looked after became simply things to be used and turned into money. It is largely irrelevant to these people if whole species of animals, plants or even native Indian tribes disappear in the process of making money. It is largely irrelevant if the earth is poisoned, if we are left with no rain-forests or even if we have holes in the ozone layer high above us.

Nothing matters to our new 'Kings' apart from accumulating wealth and power. This planet has been subjected to centuries of the most intense exploitation and is now in serious trouble. This unique and carefully balanced ecosystem which was provided for our survival and well-being has been poisoned all around us. We are about to become part of the biggest and most horrific wasteland ever known in the history of the world. Who will accept responsibility for this?

For 25,000 years the Goddess was worshipped and the earth and its people flourished. In the last 1,500 years since the Goddess religion was generally abandoned the world has changed. Millions have died and are still dying in high-tech wars. Nuclear accidents contaminate the air we breathe. Acid rain kills our forests. Untold millions perish of starvation at this very moment in time while we in Europe are actually paying farmers not to produce any more food because we cannot cope with the surplus we already have! The overriding principle which drives humanity is not the love and compassion talked about by the followers of the Christian God - that was pure propaganda. The real driving force is the accumulation of wealth and power that was made possible for men with the destruction of the matrilinear system and the abandonment of the Old Religion.

In rejecting the Goddess, men liberated themselves from the control of matrilineal society and seized power for themselves but in their greed and ambition they failed to comprehend that this control, however odious it may have seemed at times, was a very necessary part of life. It was a necessary part of life because, unfortunately, as we can see so clearly now, so many men have absolutely no control of their own. They are unable to see any further than their own immediate needs and the gratification of those needs becomes of paramount importance.

Without the guiding principle of the Goddess, Her religion and the kind of society that this gives rise to, greed and the lust for power amongst men will predominate and the end result is to be seen all around us - a wasteland for us all.

Ever since the Grail became the Holy Grail, the principle of regeneration has been lost to us. Today, however, we need it more than ever before. Will the Grail continue to be the Holy Grail, the cup of Jesus, or will it become once more a symbol of the Goddess? We must look again at the question "Whom does it serve?" Does the Grail serve the Christian God or the Goddess? If it still serves the Christian God then we can expect no regeneration. His promise to take care of things on our behalf has proved false. The process of destruction is well underway. We are sitting on a time bomb and if we are not careful we will perish in this wasteland that has been created around us. This wasteland, this poisoned earth is the only thing we have really inherited from our illustrious, greedy and power hungry forefathers.

The betrayal of Arthur has affected us all. This is why the legend will not die. This is why it does not matter where he was born or where he was buried. The legend goes beyond such trivia. Concealed within these tales is the key to the understanding of our present predicament. We must reverse Arthur's betrayal. We must look again at the principles of the Old Religion and accept anew our joint responsibility to look after the land in conjunction with the Goddess who created it. This path of the Holy Grail must be abandoned. The Grail must once more become a symbol of the Goddess so that this wasted land of ours can once again experience the magic of regeneration before it is too late.

Bíblíogrmaphy

Reference has been made in this book to the following works:

1. The Celtic Churches by John T McNeill 1974

2. The Life & Death of a Druid Prince by Anne Ross & Don Robbins 1989

3. The Celts by T.G. Powell 1980

4. The Everyday Life of the Pagan Celts by Anne Ross 1970

5. Camelot and the Vision of Albion by Geoffrey Ashe 1975

6. Celtic Bards, Chiefs and Kings by George Barrow 1928

7. Malory by Eugene Vinaver 1970

8. Arthurian Legends by Ronan Coghlan 1991

9. King Arthur and the Grail by Richard Cavendish 1978

10. King Arthur - Hero and Legend by Richard Barber 1986

11. Morte de Arthur by Thomas Malory

12. The Quest of the Holy Grail by Jessie Weston 1913

13. King Arthur and the Grail by Richard Cavendish

14. Celtic Heritage by Alwyn & Brinley Rees 1961

15. The Queen & The Cauldron by Nicholas Gold

16. When God was a Woman by Merlin Stone

17. The Greatness that was Babylon by H W Saggs 1968

18. The Origins of Britain by Lloyd & Jennifer Lang 1982

19. The Splendour That Was Egypt by Margaret Mead

20. The Twelve Olympians by Charles Seltman

21. Anglo Saxon Chronicle by Manuscript 'E'

22. The Life and Death of a Druid Priest by Ross & Robbins

23. Practical Celtic Magic by Murray Hope 1987

24. Welsh Annals by Author unknown (approx 970 AD)

25. King Arthur - the True Story by Philips & Keatman 1992

Index

Other titles from Capall Bann

A detailed illustrated catalogue is available on request, SAE or International Postal Coupon appreciated. Titles are available direct from Capall Bann, post free in the UK (cheque or PO with order) or from good bookshops and specialist outlets.

Animals, Mind Body Spirit & Folklore

Angels and Goddesses - Celtic Christianity & Paganism by Michael Howard
Arthur - The Legend Unveiled by C Johnson & E Lung
Auguries and Omens - The Magical Lore of Birds by Yvonne Aburrow
Book of the Veil The by Peter Paddon
Call of the Horned Piper by Nigel Jackson
Cats' Company by Ann Walker
Celtic Lore & Druidic Ritual by Rhiannon Ryall
Compleat Vampyre - The Vampyre Shaman: Werewolves & Witchery by Nigel Jackson
Crystal Clear - A Guide to Quartz Crystal by Jennifer Dent
Earth Dance - A Year of Pagan Rituals by Jan Brodie

Earth Magic by Margaret McArthur
Enchanted Forest - The Magical Lore of Trees by Yvonne Aburrow
Healing Homes by Jennifer Dent
Herbcraft - Shamanic & Ritual Use of Herbs by Susan Lavender & Anna Franklin
In Search of Herne the Hunter by Eric Fitch
Inner Space Workbook - Developing Counselling & Magical Skills Through the Tarot
Kecks, Keddles & Kesh by Michael Bayley
Living Tarot by Ann Walker
Magical Incenses and Perfumes by Jan Brodie
Magical Lore of Animals by Yvonne Aburrow
Magical Lore of Cats by Marion Davies

Magical Lore of Herbs by Marion Davies
Masks of Misrule - The Horned God & His Cult in Europe by Nigel Jackson
Mysteries of the Runes by Michael Howard
Oracle of Geomancy by Nigel Pennick
Patchwork of Magic by Julia Day
Pathworking - A Practical Book of Guided Meditations by Pete Jennings
Pickingill Papers - The Origins of Gardnerian Wicca by Michael Howard
Psychic Animals by Dennis Bardens
Psychic Self Defence - Real Solutions by Jan Brodie
Runic Astrology by Nigel Pennick
Sacred Animals by Gordon 'The Toad' Maclellan
Sacred Grove - The Mysteries of the Forest by Yvonne Aburrow
Sacred Geometry by Nigel Pennick
Sacred Lore of Horses The by Marion Davies
Sacred Ring - Pagan Origins British Folk Festivals & Customs by Michael Howard
Secret Places of the Goddess by Philip Heselton
Talking to the Earth by Gordon Maclellan
Taming the Wolf - Full Moon Meditations by Steve Hounsome
The Goddess Year by Nigel Pennick & Helen Field
West Country Wicca by Rhiannon Ryall
Wildwood King by Philip Kane
Witches of Oz The by Matthew & Julia Phillips

Capall Bann is owned and run by people actively involved in many of the areas in which we publish. Our list is expanding rapidly so do contact us for details on the latest releases. We guarantee our mailing list will never be released to other companies or organisations.

Capall Bann Publishing, Freshfields, Chieveley, Berks, RG20 8TF.

Celtic Lore & Druidic Ritual By Rhiannon Ryall

Inevitably the Druidic Path crosses that of any genuine Gaelic Tradition of Wicca, so this book contains much druidic lore. Background material on the Druids is also included, explaining much of their way of viewing the world & enabling the reader to understand more fully their attributions in general & their rituals in particular.

The book is divided into five parts: 1: Casting circles, seasonal sigils, wands, woods for times of the year, Celtic runes, the Great Tides, making cones & vortices of power, polarities & how to change them, the seasonal Ogham keys & Ogham correspondences. 2: Old calendar festivals & associated evocations, the "Call of Nine", two versions of the 'Six Pointed Star Dance', Mistletoe Lore, New Moon working, the Fivefold Calendar. 3: Underlying fundamentals of magical work, magical squares, the Diamond Working Area. 4: Five initiations, including a shamanic one, some minor 'calls', some 'little magics'. 5: Background information on the Celtic path, the Arthurian myth & its underlying meaning & significance, the Three Worlds of the Celts, thoughts regarding the Hidden Path & final advice.

ISBN 1 898307 225   £9.95   170 pages   Illustrated

The Sacred Ring - The Pagan Origins of British Folk Festivals & Customs
By Michael Howard

The old festivals & folk customs which are still celebrated all over the British Isles each year represent a survival of the ancient concept of a seasonal cycle based on the sacredness of the land & the earth. The progress of the year is marked in folk tradition by customs & festivals, recording the changing seasons. Some events are nominally Christian because the early church adopted many of the practices & beliefs of the pagan religions to supplant them, with little success, demonstrated by the edicts issued as late as the 11th century forbidding the wearing of animal masks & costumes, known as guising, during the Christmas festivities. All over Europe, seasonal customs & folk rituals dating from the earliest times are still celebrated. Some festivals belong to a seasonal pattern of the agricultural cycle, others record the mystical journey of the Sun across the sky, both dating back to pagan religions. Each is a unique happening combining Pagan & Christian symbolism to create seasonal celebrations which can be experienced on many different levels of understanding & enjoyment.

The Sacred Ring of the year is a reminder of our ancient past & is still a potent symbol for the 20th century. It reminds us of humankind's integral link with Nature, even in our modern technological society, which is reflected in the ritual pattern of the changing seasons of the ecological cycle.

ISBN 1 898307 28 8   £9.95   Numerous illustrations   190 pages

Inner Celtia by Alan Richardson and David Annwn

This is an experiential guide to the realm of the Celts, as it existed on the cusp between the Bronze and Iron Ages and as it still exists today in buried levels of Western consciousness. In a radical approach that turns the narrative into a vehicle for the readers ' psycho-spiritual development', "Inner Celtia" enables us to explore the strangest country of all... that which lies within. No matter what our national or racial background, no matter where we happen to live, this visionary exploration of that level of consciousness defined as Celtia can enable each person to awaken energies that they have long since lost, or locked away and which are intimately linked to that concept known as Spirit of Place.

"Inner Celtia" regards the isle of Britain, not as a geo-political entity, but as an expression of that great and dark Goddess who lies behind the Celtic experience. It further shows how we can approach this goddess by means of two figures from the 4th Century B.C., who we can enlist as guides. On one level these figures can be seen as manifestations of the anima and animus and can help us make sense of those lost and Celtic levels within the masculine and feminine consciousness. On another and overtly magical level, we can accept them as "telesmic images" or vehicles for actual spiritual guides that can put us in touch with the Celtic Otherworld.

ISBN 1 898307 520   £10.95   Nov 1995   Illustrated